'SADDA MI$$ING MILLIONS'

BY
TERRY CAVENDER

Acknowledgments:

Dedicated to my beloved wife Mags
and my precious daughter Sara.

Every effort has been
made to contact copyright holders of
any material reproduced in this book. If any have
been inadvertently overlooked, that will be rectified
at the earliest opportunity.

This book is a work of fiction.
Names, characters, businesses, organisations,
places and events are either the product of the
author's imagination or are used fictitiously.
Any resemblance to actual persons, living or
dead, or events or locales is entirely coincidental.

No part of this publication may be reproduced,
stored in or introduced into a retrieval system, or
transmitted, in any form or by any means, without
the prior permission in writing of the author, nor be
otherwise circulated in any form of binding or cover
other than that which it is published and without a
similar condition including this condition being
imposed on the subsequent purchaser.

Copyright © 2020 Terry Cavender

(The moral right of the author has been asserted)
All rights reserved.

Also by Terry Cavender:

'A BOY FROM NOWHERE'

'THREE TALL TALES'
- *It All Came Out In The Wash.*
- *Does the Führer Live?*
- *Forget Me Not.*

'THREE MORE TALL TALES'
- *T3 – The Time Tunnel.*
- *Off With His Head!*
- *Waterhouse Lane.*

'EVEN MORE TALL TALES'
- *The Bus To Bridlington.*
- *Too Old To Dream.*
- *Sup It Up!*

'ANOTHER THREE TALL TALES'
- *An Away Day In Pompeii.*
- *Excercise Burnt Toast 2.*
- *First Class!*

'BREAKING THE 4TH DIMENSION'

'TINKERING WITH TIME'

'SPYSKI'

✻✻✻

(With Harry (Brian) Clacy)
' TELL IT LIKE IT WASN'T '
(PART 1)
And
' TELL IT LIKE IT WASN'T '
(PART 2)

✻✻✻

(With Steve King)
'AS LONG AS I KNOW –
IT'LL BE QUITE ALRIGHT'

✻✻✻

'SADDAM'S MI$$ING MILLIONS'

About the Story

This story is a mixture fiction and fact – 'Faction.' Once again, the leading protagonists in this 'Time-Travel' story are: the 'dynamic-trio' - Graham St Anier, a retired Police Inspector who resides in the delightful East Yorkshire market town of Beverley, and his close friend, Kingston-Upon-Hull based Scotsman Mike Fraser, the owner of the long-established and exclusive 'Time-Travellers Incorporated' ('T2-Inc') organisation whose main offices are based in the 'Time-Travel Holiday Store' at the

Kingswood Retail Park on the outskirts of Kingston-Upon-Hull.

A fiercely proud 'Jock' - Mike Fraser is also secretly thrilled to be considered an 'Honorary' Yorkshireman.

Both Mike and Graham thrive on a spot of 'Mystery, Mischief and Mayhem.' They are joined in this new 'Time-Travel' adventure by their old friend, fellow adventurer and ex-soldier of fortune, Dutchman, Mike De Jong.

The main offices of 'T2-Inc' is where all of the 'Time-Travel' key planning and preparation takes place. Currently the only two Time-Machines – (the latest state-of-the-art 'T3-Travellators') in the world are owned and operated under strict governmental license by 'T2-Inc' and regularly 'bend time' by 'teleporting' backwards and forwards through time from Humberside Travelport where 'T2-Inc' has its own closely guarded, government approved secure hangar facility.

The intrepid 'Time-Traveller Team' hurtles through the ether in their 'T3-Travellator' across to the high security compound at Moscow's Sheremetyevo Airport where ex-President Saddam Hussein has stashed away many billions of American dollars with the Russians for safe-keeping.

The lads plan to relieve Saddam of some of those dollars.

During the course of their 'visit' they bump into arch- enemies, the Russian FSB's much-feared General Igor Chelpinsky and his evil cohort Colonel Ivanski Gregorovitch, and that's when all hell breaks loose.

This is the 'Time-Team's' most daring undertaking yet.

CHAPTERS

Introduction.

1. Time to Move On!

2. Shock and Awe.

3. The '*OP EXTRACTION*' Plan.

4. The Compound.

5. Breaking and Entering.

6. Tally Ho!

7. The Comrade Supreme Commander requires your presence!

8. Nearly There.

9. The Saint Petersburg Compound.

10. Escape and Evasion.

11. Heading for Home.

12. All is Safely Gathered In.

13. The Break-through.

14. Back to Iraq.

15. To the Rescue.

16. Time To Go Home.

17. The Zelnograd Mortuary.

18. So What's Next?

19. No Place Like Home.

20. Cheerio Chelpinski.

21. Down at the old 'Dog and Duck.'

Ж

'SADDAM'S MISSING MILLIONS'

Introduction:

Saddam Hussein Abd al-Majid al-Tikriti was the President of Iraq from July 1979 until April 2003, when his time expired and he was executed. For several years before his elevation to President, Saddam had already been the 'de facto' head of Iraq so was a force to be reckoned with.

He had been a very brutal dictator and it is believed that the total number of Iraqis slaughtered by his government during various purges and genocides was somewhere in the region of a quarter of a million innocents.

His invasions of Iran and Kuwait also resulted in many thousands of deaths. Saddam Hussein's power throughout the period of his reign was absolute.

'President Saddam Hussein Abd al-Majid al-Tikriti'
High Excellency, Field Marshal & Commander of all Iraq'

Things came to a head for Saddam, however, in 2003 when a mighty coalition, led by the United States of America, invaded Iraq and toppled both Saddam and his Ba'ath Party. The Ba'ath Party was then disbanded and 'free' elections were held.

Saddam, who had slunk off into hiding, was eventually captured on the 13th of December 2003, after being betrayed and was found skulking in a hidden underground pit outside the town of Ad-Dawara, on the outskirts of Tikrit, as a result of an American military security operation, 'OPERATION RED DAWN.'

An exhausted and frightened Saddam capitulated without putting up a fight.

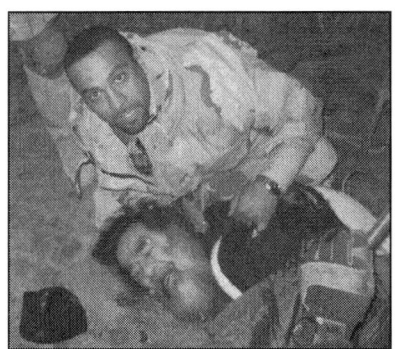

*'US Army photo of the capture of
'President Saddam Hussein'*

Towards the end of the invasion, when coalition bombs were raining down on the Iraqi capital, the President's son, Qusay Hussein and Abid al-Hamid Mahmood, Saddam's Personal Assistant, along with five other Presidential 'officials' withdrew nearly $1 billion dollars from the Nation's Central Bank, using flat-bed trucks to transport the money out of Baghdad and then on to a secret location.

The removal had been authorised by President Saddam personally, prior to his downfall. Only a few key people were told where the money was being taken to. It is believed that the intention was to use these ill-gotten gains to fund the President's escape and also to help him and his family survive once he'd been removed from power.

The money amounted to roughly a quarter of the Iraqi Central Bank's hard currency reserves. In addition to that, about $400 million American dollars and a huge *amount of Iraqi currency was also taken by looters from various banks across the country, most of which disappeared into thin air.*

After his capture, the ex-President was placed on trial front of an Iraqi Special Tribunal where he was found guilty of crimes against humanity and sentenced to death by hanging.

Like one of his hero's, Germany's Hermann Göering, Saddam requested that he be executed by firing squad, which, like Göering, was denied. He was to be hanged and that was the end of the matter.

Early on the morning of the 30th of December 2006, Saddam ate his last meal, his favourite - chicken and rice, washed down with a cup of hot water and honey, before being executed at the joint Iraqi-American base, the aptly named Camp Justice, in Iraq.

It has long been rumoured that a fortune in unclaimed American dollars is stored in a closely guarded high security area tucked safely away inside Moscow's huge Sheremetyevo Airport. It is believed to have been stored there on behalf of Saddam Hussein whilst he was still in a position of authority.

On closer investigation, the money appears to have been transported, under conditions of great secrecy, to Moscow - from somewhere in the Arab Emirates.

It is also claimed that there are up to 200 one-ton wooden pallets containing many billions of American dollars stacked up in Sheremetyevo Airport's High Security Compound and that it belongs to a so far untraceable individual named 'Ferzan Mollags.'

The Russian Intelligence Agencies took control and overall responsibility for the shipment and so there it sits in the compound - (which is purportedly as safe as Fort Knox), under constant armed guard, waiting to be collected by 'Ferzan' - when the time is ripe.

FERZAN   MOLLAGS   -   SADDAM   HUSSEIN
6 letters   7 letters   -   6 letters   7 letters

(Just saying - Author)

CHAPTER ONE

'TIME TO MOVE ON!'

Totally laid-back, ignoring all of the mayhem swirling around him, and despite the never ending series of nerve-shattering thuds from exploding bombs, a completely unconcerned and bored looking President Saddam Hussein was sat, suede desert boots planted on his magnificent desk, lounging back in his finely tooled leather desk chair, a chair that had original been the property of the Emir of Kuwait until Saddam had claimed it for himself as a war trophy.

The President's air-conditioned office was relatively quiet, apart from those occasional sound of distant explosions that filtered through the heavily reinforced ceiling and walls. All of the windows had been boarded up to prevent the chance of the President being injured by flying glass. He hadn't been too pleased at the time, but was persuaded that his personal safety was of prime concern to his general staff.

Saddam was idly twirling a gold-plated 9mm Glock 18c pistol around his forefinger, rather like a gunslinger in a cheap 'B' western movie.

The gold pistol was one of several such weapons that had been presented to him by various feather-bedding Heads of State who wished to curry favour with the President, back when Saddam was still a force to contend with in the middle-east.

Mounted on the wall behind the Dictator's desk was an eye-catching, glittering gold-plated AK-47 rifle, just one of several that had been gifted to Saddam and he'd proudly ordered to be displayed on the walls around his various palaces.

Stood directly in front of Saddam's desk, and in direct line of fire should the Glock go off, was his 'body-double,' an apprehensive and quivering Akram Shamoon. Akram was praying fervently to Allah that the safety catch on the President's spinning pistol was switched onto the safe mode.

The resemblance between Saddam Hussein and Akram Shamoon was startling and it was said that the only time anyone, even some of Saddam's close family members, could tell the difference between the two of them was when the Presidential Bodyguards accompanying the President were seen to be relaxed, laughing and joking.

The laughter and joking indicated to those in the know that it was Akram Shamoon and not President Saddam Hussein himself that they were protecting. The Presidential Bodyguard would not have dared to laugh and joke in the presence of the real, murderous and very vindictive President. He would have had them dismissed and shot out of hand, and they knew that.

The body-double, Akram Shamoon, purported, in public anyway, to worship and adore his President and had sworn to willingly lay down his life for him. In reality his adoration was just a way for Akram to stay in the President's good books and also help him continue to earn a good living, and one for which he was paid handsomely. Another perk of the job was that he was given the President's very expensive cast-off clothing and footwear.

Akram didn't know it then, but the 'voluntary' option of throwing himself on his sword was now out of his hands. Akram Shamoon was pencilled-in by Saddam to be a 'sacrificial lamb.' If the coalition forces didn't get Akram, then the Presidential Bodyguard would.

Before that happened, the President's intention was that Akram would go on the run, popping up in different places, thereby confusing his enemies as to Saddam's precise whereabouts.

It had also been made quite clear to Akram that under no circumstances was he to allow himself to be captured alive by the coalition forces or anyone else for that matter. He was expected to fight to the bitter end, then if his capture looked imminent, he was ordered to kill himself.

After his suicide, Akram's body would then be 'found' and the coalition forces, wrongly, would assume that it was the real Saddam Hussein. Saddam himself would by that stage be heading out of Iraq like a rat scuttling up a drainpipe.

Were Akram to attempt to change his mind and renege on his agreement by deciding not to commit suicide, the Presidential Bodyguard accompanying him at all times had been instructed to ease him off the side.

Akram had made a pact with the Devil, choosing to ignore the adage that *'He who sups with the Devil should have a long spoon.'* Que será, será, Goodbye Akram.

Everything had been planned to give the impression that Saddam Hussein had been defiant and heroically fought the coalition forces right up to the very end, so under no circumstances could Akram be captured alive to prove otherwise.

In the meantime, Saddam and his immediate family would show Iraq a clean pair of heels as they flew off to safety using his two personal jets, cram-packed with whatever riches they could manage.

Unusually for him, that day Saddam was dressed in 'civvies' and not wearing one of the many splendid, colourful and beautifully tailored military uniforms that he usually favoured.

To all intents and purposes, apart from the civilian attire, it could have been just another day at the office, but the President had readied himself to move out at a moment's notice. If and when that happened, he needed to be low profile, thus the civilian clothing.

As the President was speaking to Akram, in the background they could both clearly hear the sound of enemy jet aircraft, their engines howling across the skies of down-town Baghdad as they swooped over, dropping their deadly loads on various key military targets.

It was proving difficult for the coalition pilots, not only because they were coming under very heavy fire, but because they knew that Saddam had given orders for several key military installations and command headquarters to be hidden away underneath schools and hospitals and other such sensitive buildings. The general concepts of the Geneva Convention just didn't figure in Saddam Hussein's plans or conscience.

Every few minutes there was the booming sound of yet more coalition bombs exploding, usually followed by the spine-chilling whooshing of rockets being launched from coalition air force jets at specific targets and at anything on the ground resembling a military target, static or otherwise.

There was no quarter given by the coalition forces.

The constant hellish cacophony of sound was interspersed with the now sporadic and greatly weakened return fire from the Iraqi Ground Defence Forces, who were hammering away with their anti-aircraft cannons and heavy machine guns, gun-crews frantically firing at the incoming aircraft with, apparently, very little demonstrable positive effect. Unfortunately for the Iraqi's, they were fast running out of ammunition.

If anything, despite the Iraqi Ground Defence Forces desperate defensive efforts, the volume and accuracy of incoming destructive ordnance was increasing by the hour and was overwhelming them. The Iraqi Air Force, what was left of it, was nowhere to be seen. It was just a matter of time before the Iraqi's were completely overcome.

It didn't take the brains of an Ayatollah to work out that the battle for Baghdad, and by exception Iraq, was rapidly drawing to a conclusion and that it was a battle that Saddam and his henchmen knew they couldn't and wouldn't win.

The self-centred President had already decided that it was time for him to fold his tents and disappear over the horizon to safety. He planned to live to fight another day. The ongoing loss of life in Iraq, however, would continue as Saddam had decided not to instructed his armed forces to surrender during the interim period. The unnecessary slaughter that this would cause didn't concern Saddam one iota because as far as he was concerned, his soldiers were just cannon fodder.

He didn't give a second thought about the loss of life, just as long as he and his immediate family were safe, that's all that mattered to Saddam.

Unlike another one of his all-time heroes, Adolf Hitler, Saddam had secretly decided, despite all of his macho speeches to the contrary, that he wasn't prepared to make a final heroic stand against the coalition forces from the Presidential 'bunker' inside which he was currently skulking and sulking.

Saddam knew full well what would happen to him and the key members of his close family if they had the misfortune to fall into enemy hands, albeit coalition or the more home-grown opposition - and that what happened to them wouldn't be a pretty sight.

He'd decided that under no circumstances must either he or his family would be taken prisoner, or more to the point - taken alive. To that end they had all been issued with suicide pills.

Saddam often recalled with horror what had happened to the Italian dictator Benito Mussolini when he and his mistress, Claretta Petacci, had been captured by Italian partisans then put against a wall and executed by firing squad on the 28th of April 1945, after which their bodies were put on public display, hung like animal's carcasses in a butchers shop for all to see. Their bodies had been jeered and spat at whilst the whole sordid event was captured on film for all the world to see.

(The demise of Italian Dictator Benito Mussolini and his mistress, Claretta Petacci – 29th April 1945)

It hadn't been a pretty sight and Saddam was determined that he wouldn't let anything like that happen to him or his family.

Saddam wasn't overly concerned about being captured by the coalition forces, but he was well aware that there were many of his own people thirsting for his blood and that they would be seeking revenge for the various cruelties and outrages that he and his cohorts had committed against them during the years that he'd held the reins of power.

He knew full well that various factions within Iraq wanted to get their hands on him before the coalition forces could. If they succeeded he knew that the very least he could expect was to be abused, beaten then torn limb from limb.

With animal cunning, which he possessed in spades, Saddam had realised many months before that he had overstayed his welcome in Iraq, long before it became a subject of hushed public discussion.

In view of that, he had decided to grab whatever riches he could and make a swift, covert exit when precisely the right time came. He'd reached the conclusion that the moment had now arrived.

Saddam understood that he had no other option than to leave his beloved Iraq, but was resolute that he would return in due course and regain what he considered to be his rightful position as Head of the Iraqi State, no matter how long it took him. Until then, he was determined to live on to fight another day,

On his eventual return to Iraq he had already made plans to set about wreaking a terrible revenge upon those whom he considered had plotted and schemed to bring about his downfall. They and their families would suffer horrible deaths.

Saddam already had a list of suspects, some of whom had already been dealt with in the most cruel of fashions, the others would have to wait, but Saddam was determined that their time would come. He had a long memory and was a vindictive man.

As Saddam began speaking to his body-double Akram, there was a particularly thunderous explosion. The huge and ostentatious Swarovsky chrystal chandelier that usually filled the room with warm light, rattled, flickered and swayed then suddenly went out, leaving Saddam's desk lamp as the only source of light in the room.

In the half-light cast out by the lamp, Saddam's sallow features took on a positively satanic demeanour, unsettling Akram even more.

The walls of the room shook and a layer of fine white dust floated down from the arched ceiling onto the President's highly polished desk. Akram visibly flinched, but Saddam didn't bat an eyelid, convinced that he was invincible. A fear-stricken Akram, unable to control himself, farted noisily, causing Saddam to wrinkle his nose in disgust, thinking, *"Disgusting, spineless creature."*

Under normal circumstances, Akram would have received a severe beating for such outrageous and disrespectful behaviour in the presence of the President.

"Fear not, my brother, no harm will come to us" said Saddam, *"remember that we have several feet of the finest reinforced Russian concrete both around us and over our heads to provide protection. Let me assure you that we are perfectly safe in here."*

Saddam looked across at the badly frightened Akram and thought, rather uncharitably, *"Huh, look at him, trembling like a jelly! Cowards die many times before their death. The valiant never taste death but once."*

It hadn't occurred to Saddam that whilst he was busy denigrating lesser mortals, he'd made plans to abandon his own sinking ship without so much as a second thought.

Nodding towards an ornate throne-like chair directly in front of his desk, Saddam waved his hand imperiously towards it and commanded, *"Be seated and rest your trembling legs, Akram; you are beginning to make your President nervous. Quickly now, I have matters to discuss with you that cannot wait."*

A relieved Akram sat down then waited patiently for the pearls of wisdom that were about to pour forth from his beloved President's mouth. *"Now,"* said Saddam, *"let us tidy up a few final details!"*

Wishing that the President would get his arse in gear, Akram was getting twitchy because all he wanted to do was to get out of the palace, desert his post and scuttle off back home to his family.

Akram had already decided that the first thing he was going to do once he reached home was to get rid of the presidential uniforms, shave off his bushy moustache and rinse the black dye out of his hair. The last thing he wanted was to look anything like President Saddam Hussein.

Even Akram, not the brightest of individuals, had figured out that the Saddam Hussein body-double game was well and truly up.

Once his moustache and hair dye had been dispensed with and he was back to wearing civilian clothing, Akram was convinced that as only his immediate family and friends knew how he'd earned his living, then they would be happy to cover for him until things quietened down.

After all, over the years that Saddam had been in power, Akram had managed to keep his family out of harms way and in the luxury to which they'd soon become accustomed.

Unfortunately for Akram, he wouldn't be allowed to go home. President Hussein had other plans for him.

Saddam took a deep breath, then began speaking. *"I have summoned you here today, Akram Shamoon, because I wish to discuss something of great importance with you!"* he said. *"You must pay strict attention as this could well be the last time we meet."*

*"Earlier this year you and I, attended several highly classified briefings regarding the complex procedures for the implementation of the highly sensitive **'OPERATION DOUBLE-DIAMOND'** - is that not so?"*

Akram nodded respectfully and replied, *"With respect, that is correct, Your Excellency."*

The President continued, *"Well, the time has now arrived for the operation to be activated. You know from those briefings precisely what is required of you and I am relying upon you to carry out your instructions to the letter."* Akram was like a nodding dog.

Saddam continued, *"You will, of course, be well rewarded for your valiant efforts, Akram, and in the unlikely event that things should not go as planned and you fall in battle, then you can rest assured that your family will never want for anything again. You have my personal guarantee on that."*

Nervously wringing his hands, Akram was trembling and starting to sweat, despite the air-conditioning that was, surprisingly, still working and humming away in the background. Fortunately the palace had its own generators.

Akram replied, ingratiatingly, *"Mister President, please permit me to assure you that my miserable life is yours to do with as you wish ..."*

Saddam held his hands up, palms facing Akram, *"My brother, I appreciate that you are dedicated to making the ultimate sacrifice - if that should ever become necessary, but I don't believe that it is ever likely to happen. Trust me."*

Saddam smiled, causing Akram to perspire even more. *"Fortunately,"* continued Saddam, *"we are always one step ahead of those who wish to do us harm, in particular those stupid American dogs - who, as we all know, don't know their arses from their elbows."*

A fawning Akram replied, *"It has been and always will be a great honour to serve you, in whatever capacity, and I have every faith in your judgement, Your Excellency. I will fight at your side until you tell me otherwise,"* trying his best to sound a lot braver than he currently felt.

Saddam Hussein nodded and smiled again. Akram shivered involuntarily and thought that Saddam's hooded brooding eyes made him look just like those of a fearsome crocodile surfacing from the murky depths, its jaws about to snap shut on the juicy and unsuspecting body of an innocent swimmer.

Pausing momentarily, Saddam sucked disconcertingly on his highly polished gleaming white teeth then said to Akram, *"Once we have finished here, you will be escorted from the palace by members of my Presidential Bodyguard and driven over to the 'Domes Palace' where you are to remain for one evening only."*

"After that," Saddam continued, *"and for the forseeable future, you will switch alternatively between the 'Domes' and the 'Victory over America' Palaces. That is a course of action which my enemies would expect of me and will continue to sow the seeds of their confusion. Is that clearly understood?"*

Akram nodded, *"I am yours to command, Excellency."*

Akram knew that Saddam much preferred the facilities of the Domes Palace to any of the several other extremely well-appointed palaces available to him, primarily because, along with every other luxury, it had a fully equipped 'en-suite' torture chamber within spitting distance of the President's plush private quarters.

The frequently used torture facility was, as far as Saddam was concerned, like a bathroom - simply a matter of convenience, and he'd spent many happy hours watching and listening to the cruel and bestial proceedings that took place there on virtually a daily basis, even when he himself wasn't present.

Akram never fully understood how the President could fornicate with his mistresses then sleep comfortably in a bedroom where right next door there was a blood-stained hell on earth, a custom designed torture chamber; one with well stacked shelves of fearsome surgical instruments and other ghoulish pieces of custom designed torture equipment, the mere sight of which would be guaranteed to turn a victims bowels to ice.

No expense had been spared on the torture chamber's construction and equipment. In the centre of the well lit room there was a fully kitted out surgical operating table and at its side a modern dentists chair. Saddam took a perverse delight in watching innocent victims, usually naked, being strapped into the dental chair and watching their horrified faces as they heard the sound of the dental drill being cranked up. For some perverse reason the sound of horrified victims begging for mercy made Saddam laugh hysterically.

He could and often did view the torture proceedings via a two-way mirror mounted on the wall adjacent to his bed, often forcing his mistresses to watch with him.

Saddam would have his staff pour a balloon of the finest cognac for him, then he'd light up one of his favourite cheroots, chuckling as the torturers did their work. The louder the victims screamed, the louder the President laughed and evidently the more he enjoyed himself.

The President happily 'bloodied' his own hands on those being tortured, but in the main he took great enjoyment watching the proceedings through the mirror. On the rare occasions that he became bored by the proceedings, he would give the order for the mercifully swift 'despatch' of the poor unfortunate victim.

He had been known to storm into the torture chamber and take over the proceedings if things weren't going to his satisfaction. Saddam was an experienced dab hand at torture and prided himself in his 'expertise.'

It also gave Saddam a vicarious thrill knowing that his mistress was viewing the proceedings through the two-way mirror.

Giving Akram a faux-friendly and lop-sided grin, Saddam said, *"Now, you had better be on your way, my brother. The Chief of Staff will contact you in the very near future with further instructions. Remember what I have told you, and obey only him and no-one else, is that clear?"*

Akram, not daring to interrupt, nodded to indicate that he understood.

Saddam continued, *"In the highly unlikely event that you think you are about to fall into enemy hands and taken prisoner, you know what is required of you. You are to fight to the bitter end, as would I. If all else fails, you will be expected to use the suicide pill that I know you have been issued with. I am depending on you!"*

A trembling Akram, deciding that a response was necessary, said, *"I have sworn very many times that I will willingly lay down my life for you, your Excellency."* In a fit of misplaced patriotic enthusiasm, Akram surprised Saddam by leaping to his feet and begging, *"May I have the honour of kissing your sacred hand, Mister President?"*

A nodding Saddam thought, *"Akram, you dim-witted son of a camel, you can kiss my arse for all I care. It matters not, your days on this earth are numbered."*

Saddam held out his hand, then Akram bent forward and brushed his lips across the back of it. Akram noticed that despite his stoic demeanour, the President's slightly podgy and nicotine stained fingers were trembling slightly. The pressure was even beginning to get to Saddam.

"Ultimate victory will be yours, Excellency, you are truly a giant amongst lesser men," said Akram, now in fawning overdrive.

Face impassive, Saddam nodded in agreement, whilst in reality he was thinking, *"Ah, Akram, will you never learn that it is better to remain silent and be thought a fool than to open your mouth and remove all doubt."*

Saddam sighed and commanded, *"You may leave me now!"* imperiously waving Akram away before dabbing the back of his hand with a silk handkerchief to remove the beads of spittle from where Akram had kissed it. Saddam then dropped the silk handkerchief into a metal waste basket.

A greatly relieved Akram bowed his head, then turned and scuttled out of the Presidential office, away from the evil presence of his glorious leader for what he sincerely hoped and prayed would be for the very last time. Even Akram, not the brightest star in the firmament, appreciated that the end of Saddam's reign was nigh.

Akram didn't know it at that precise moment, but his dearest wish would be granted - he would not see his beloved President, Saddam Hussein, ever again.

On his way out of the palace, Akram had the misfortune to bump into Saddam's malevolent number two son, Qusay Hussein, who was on his way to see his father. Akram quickly side-stepped Qusay, saluted him then bowed his head respectfully.

As Qusay strode past, Akram said a respectful. *"Good morning, Your Excellency!"* Qusay stopped and stared at him.

The vile and unpredictable Qusay had been known to execute people for not paying him the requisite amount of respect and the expected obeisance, (as one unfortunate senior Iraqi military officer had discovered when he failed to salute Qusay and was pistol-whipped on the spot as a result).

After his prolonged beating, the unfortunate officer also had his brains blown out by an enraged, uncontrollable and unaccountable Qusay.

When his doting father, the President had been informed about the incident, he'd just tutted and laughed, putting it down to Qusay being a little over-enthusiastic in his duties. Saddam had commented, *"The boy is high spirited! What else would you expect him to do?"* No-one dared to complain and the matter was left there.

With steely, souless eyes, Qusay glanced dismissively at his father's body-double and half-heartedly returned Akram's salute, thinking, *"Baboon!"* then, much to Akram's relief, without saying another word, Qusay turned and strutted off. Akram, delighted and relieved to be away from Qusay's evil and ominous presence, went to find the Presidential Bodyguard, as instructed.

As Akram made his way along the palaces marble-lined passages he noted that the sound of explosions from outside were getting more frequent. The bombing was reaching lunatic proportions, one explosion rolling into the other.

"If the bombing continues at this rate for very much longer there won't be a single building left standing in Baghdad. I hope that my dear wife and family are safe," thought Akram.

Before Qusay was allowed to enter his father's office, the officer in charge of the four heavily armed soldiers guarding the doorway had politely requested Qusay to hand over his pistol, which had annoyed him, but nevertheless he handed it over.

He couldn't really refuse to do so as it was a Presidential Directive that the only person permitted to have a loaded weapon whilst in the President's office was the President himself.

"Have that cleaned and checked whilst I am with the President. I will collect it on my way out!" ordered a spiteful Qusay as he passed his pistol to the officer in charge of the 'gate-guard' who nodded deferentially, whilst thinking, *"Arrogant little shite-hawk!"*

Striding into the office, and without being invited to, Qusay threw himself into the chair in front of his Father's desk, recently vacated by Akram. Qusay was one of only a very few people who would dare to sit down without permission from the President himself.

"Well, what news do you bring me, my son?" asked Saddam. *"Your personal aircraft has been refuelled and is stood-by waiting for your arrival at Saddam*

International Airport, precisely as per your instructions, my beloved father," replied Qusay.

Qusay smiled and continued, *"It has had every trace of its presidential livery removed and has been repainted to emulate the markings of a Red Cross aircraft, as has the second aircraft that we are also using for the escape and evasion plan."*

"Your dear wife Samaira, and my sisters Raghad, Hala and Rana, accompanied by their families, are at the airport and are on board the first aircraft, awaiting your arrival."

"The remainder of our family, including myself and brother Uday, will follow on in the second aircraft, once we have been informed that you have left Iraqi airspace."

"Incidentally, Qusay, where is that rascal Uday at the moment?" asked Saddam. *"He's out and about settling a few scores before we leave Iraq, Father. I told him that it wasn't important, but he insisted,"* said Qusay.

Saddam shook his head sorrowfully, *"That boy will be the death of me. Make sure that he gets to the airport in plenty of time will you. You know how to handle him,"* he said. Qusay nodded and said, *"I will do my best, father."*

Saddam continued, *"And what are the arrangements for my Parisoula?"* (Parisoula Lamapsos was Saddam's long-time mistress).

"*After we were informed by the Mukhabarat (*) that her movements were being closely monitored by enemies of the state, father, I ordered that she be moved immediately by road to the safe house in Al Aubar.*"

(*) Mukhabarat - (Jihaz Al-Mukhabarat Al-Amma), the General Directorate of Iraqi Intelligence).

"*Parisoula was accompanied to the house by a small but very efficient armed escort in the early hours of this morning. She will be closely guarded whilst there, father. I personally informed the guards that their continued existence depends upon Parisoula remaining unharmed,*" said Qusay.

Saddam nodded, "*Excellent. We Husseins need to look after ourselves and those close to us.*" He sighed, "*The clock is ticking and time is now of the essence.*" As he was speaking, the faint sound of small-arms fire could be heard in the background.

Qusay glanced down at his ultra-expensive Rolex Daytona jewel encrusted, solid gold watch, (rumoured to have been once owned by the American actor Paul Newman), and said, "*Later on today, Parisoula will be moved safely across the Iraq border to another of our safe houses. I will receive a confirmatory 'phone call to that effect and will let you or your Chief of Staff know at the earliest opportunity, father. You have enough to concern yourself with. I will take care of everything.*"

Saddam nodded, *"Yes, you must let us know immediately. As you are aware, I am very fond of Parisoula, Qusay, and would not wish to see any harm befall her."*

"I assure you that she will not come to any harm, father, you have my word on that," said a confident Qusay. *"Well, if she should be, then it will be your cock that will be on the block, as the vulgar Americans say!"* said a smiling Saddam.

Inwardly cringing at his father's veiled threat, Qusay couldn't decide if he meant it or not. The odds were, though, that he did.

Qusay had ensured that many palms had been greased with a great amount of (other people's) money to ensure that Parisoula could get out of Iraq safely and would eventually reach her ultimate destination, Moscow.

Moscow was where the President and his cohorts were heading, once they had 'abandoned' the ship of state and a decimated Iraq, along with whatever money and valuables they could take with them.

Having also made all of the necessary reception arrangements with the FSB (the Russian Security Service), Qusay knew that he would be expected to continue doling out even more money to the Russians once he arrived in Moscow and for some time after that. They were like sparrows in the nest waiting for feeding time.

Money was the very least of the Hussein family problems. They'd had the foresight to stash away breathtaking amounts of money and valuables in various safe havens for many years previously, in the event that they had to cut and run. Stripping Kuwait of everything of value had been the icing on the cake.

"Parisoula will meet up with you in Moscow in a few days, father," said Qusay confidently, *"I personally guarantee that."* Qusay could never quite understand his father's fascination with Parisoula and had often thought to himself when looking at her, *"You can put lipstick on a pig, but it's still a pig."* Unlike Qusay, Saddam preferred his women to have a bit of meat on their bones.

Reaching across and patting Qusay on the shoulder, Saddam said, *"As expected, you have done well, my dear son. You are one of the very few people that I can totally rely upon to get a job done. I wish that we'd had a few more like you surrounding me!"*

Sighing contentedly, Saddam continued, *" How I love it when a good plan comes together. Now, my son, about the all important subject of money. Put my mind at rest and tell me that everything is in order in that respect?"*

Qusay nodded, *"Yes father, I can assure you that it is. Once we have finished speaking here, for instance, I am heading straight for the State Bank. I will be accompanied by Abid al-Hamid Mahmood and a small escort of the Presidential Bodyguard."*

"Abid has already arranged for the 'withdrawal' of the final one billion dollars, American, and for it to be trucked away to the secret location, precisely as we agreed."

Saddam nodded and said, *"Excellent. As my father, your beloved grand-father used to say - 'Let us put hay in the barn whilst we can!' Which was quite amusing as we didn't even have a barn at the time."*

A smiling Qusay continued, *"At the pre-arranged location, once the money has been cross-loaded and is ready to be moved on, as per standard procedure - the bodyguards and drivers accompanying us will then be executed and replaced, thus removing that link in the chain of information."*

"And the onwards transmission of the money to Moscow?" asked Saddam.

"That is well in hand, Father." said Qusay, *" As you directed, the money will be taken by an Iraqi freight ship to Saint Petersburg where it will then be unloaded and moved overland, accompanied by an FSB escort, to the secure location in Moscow."*

"As agreed with the FSB, it will be disguised throughout as urgent medical supplies. I must tell you that President Baronovski's staff could not have been more helpful. It's almost as if they've done this sort of thing before," said Qusay.

Saddam smiled knowingly and tapped his bulbulous, red veined nose with a well manicured forefinger, *"They have, my son, many times and for many other people too."*

He sighed, *"However, always bear in mind that the Russians are not to be trusted, Qusay. President Baronovski, although a dear friend, is attracted to money like iron filings to a magnet!"* *"Trust me, father,"* said Qusay, *"all will be well."*

After a few seconds pause Saddam continued, *"There comes a time, my son, when one can no longer cling to the wreckage and that time, in my view, has arrived,"* he sighed heavily before continuing. *"Very well, I have listened closely to what you have just told me and I think that it is now time for* **'OPERATION DOUBLE-DIAMOND'** *to begin!"*

Qusay nodded, *"Everything has been prepared for your departure, father. Your armoured Mercedes is waiting, with an armed escort, outside the concealed exit at the rear of the palace to take you directly to the airport. We have had the surrounding area cleared to ensure that no-one will witness you leaving here."*

He continued, *"Once you have flown away from the airport and the second aircraft has taken off, those men that escorted us there and those in the aircraft tower monitoring our departure will be replaced immediately and executed. There will be no witnesses left alive to let the cat out of the bag,"* said Qusay.

Saddam nodded his approval. "*Good, that is good. We must keep our enemies floundering around in the dark for as long as possible,*" said Saddam.

Saddam was inordinately proud of Qusay, who he considered was a most reliable son, the complete opposite of his totally lunatic brother, the loose cannon Uday. Uday was a totally different kettle of fish and was, alas, more like his father in temperament, so needed to be handled with kid gloves at all times. Both Saddam and his son Uday were sadistic rapists with incredibly short fuses.

Uday had never been the same since an assassination attempt when he had been badly wounded by gunfire. As a result of there being an inoperable bullet lodged near his spine, he was in constant pain. The unending pain had tipped him completely over the brink and now he was bordering on being completely uncontrollable and unpredictable. It hadn't helped that Uday thought his own brother Qusay was involved in the attempt, but he he no evidence to prove it.

Saddam and Qusay had realised long ago that Uday was a suitable case for treatment and had arranged to have him admitted to one of the best psychiatric hospitals in Moscow at the earliest opportunity after their arrival in Russia. Uday couldn't be allowed to roam freely, it would inevitably end in tears.

If the Russian psychiatric treatment didn't work, Saddam was seriously considering having Uday locked away in an institution where, for the rest of his life, he could be left to howl at the moon to his heart's content.

As Qusay stood up to leave, Saddam said, "*Oh, there is just one other small matter, Qusay!*" "*There is something I have neglected to do, father?*" asked Qusay.

Pointing towards the door, Saddam asked, "*The immediate family of my body-double, Akram Shamoon. Have they been dealt with in accordance with my instructions?*"

Qusay nodded, "*Yes indeed, father. They were arrested, then taken away to be executed and disposed of late last night, exactly as per your wishes.*"

Saddam nodded approvingly and smiled. "*Good boy, well done. You have an excellent eye for detail!*" he said, "*It's the little things that matter in life.*" Qusay smiled, "*If heads have to roll, it is my job to ensure that the baskets are ready, father!*" Saddam laughed at that.

"*Are you going to collect Uday then?* asked Saddam. Qusay nodded, "*Yes, father. He will be accompanying us to the bank.*" Saddam smiled, "*Good, good. You know, you two remind me very much of myself when I was your age. Now, be off with you. I will see you both soon – and stay safe!*" "*You don't need to worry about me, father,*" said a smiling Qusay.

After Qusay had departed, Saddam stood up, stretched then confidently holstered his pistol. He, more than anyone else, knew full well that the time had come for him to step off the international stage - just for the moment anyway. He was determined that he would be back.

It was beyond doubt that the hated coalition forces would do their utmost to try and capture him alive and then place him on a show-trial, and that's when his body-double Akram Shamoon, would then come into the picture. Shamoon would not know that his family had been eliminated so would soldier on and do his duty.

The real Saddam would be long gone and preparing for a life of luxury somewhere on the outskirts of Moscow, plotting, scheming and marshalling his forces.

Akram Shamoon had been well briefed regarding the Presidential deception and would continue in his role for as long as humanly possible. If captured he'd been instructed to crunch down on the cyanide capsule that had been secreted inside one of his molars by Saddam's personal dentist. The enemy would not, could not be given the opportunity to beat the truth out of him.

In the very unlikely event that he was captured alive, Akram had been instructed to refuse to answer any of his captors questions for at least forty eight hours. He was to remain silent - or else those close to him would suffer!

Despite his never-ending protestations of undying loyalty, Akram had decided long ago that if he was captured by the enemy, bugger biting down on the poison capsule, he would immediately confess to being a 'body-double' and then eventually, when everything had quitened down, would, hopefully, be allowed to return unharmed to the bosom of his family and resume a normal life.

"After all," Akram told himself, *" I personally haven't done anything wrong, other than acting as a body-double for the President, and where's the crime in that? All I ever did was wave and smile. I'm not going to get executed for that!"*

Akram was also confident that post-Saddam, there could be a good living to be made in personal appearances, in the theatre and possibly in movies, opening supermarkets, acting as a double for the ex-President, after the war.

Although he knew what was expected of him, Akram had absolutely no intention whatsoever of committing suicide and had secretly arranged for his own dentist to remove the cyanide capsule from his hollowed out tooth and replace it with a dummy one.

"Why should I take the long drop!" Akram had thought, *"All I did was to literally play a part - and I had no choice in the matter. Anyway, I would have been shot out of hand had I refused."*

Meanwhile, as Akram headed off for the Domes Palace, the elaborate security precautions that had been made for Saddam Hussein and his cohorts to fly out of the beleaguered Saddam International Airport began kicking in. Saddam had emptied his wall safe and was heading for the palace exit for what was probably the final time.

The two illegally disguised private jets that were waiting to take off and fly on to the safety of Moscow, by a circuitous route, well away from the prying eyes of satellites, had their engines cranked up and spinning in readiness for the President and his party to arrive.

Saddam's aircraft would take off the instant he boarded. There was not a second to waste.

Both jets, as his son Qusay had informed him, had had their original Presidential livery removed and were then repainted so that they now resembled International Red Cross aircraft and would expect to be treated as such by the international community, particularly the ever-present coalition aircraft.

Needless to say, the unfortunate team of technicians that had carried out the respraying jobs would not be using paint sprayers ever again. As soon as their work had been completed they had been taken away to a nearby hangar, stood up against a wall and gunned down, their bodies thrown into the back of a covered truck and taken out into the desert for burial.

As planned, Saddam's aircraft would be the first to leave, then the second similarly camouflaged aircraft carrying the remainder of Saddam's close relatives and a few other favoured members of his command staff would follow on shortly after that.

Like the first aircraft, the second one was crammed from floor to ceiling with gold, jewellery, precious artefacts and many other valuables that had been pilfered over the years. There was hardly a bar of gold left in the central Iraqi bank. It would take the Iraq economy many years to recover, but that was the least of Saddam's worries.

Once he had clambered onboard his aircraft and it had taken off, Saddam unbuckled his seat belt and turned to a remarkably pretty, leggy French Stewardess. Peering at her name-badge he silkily instructed her to, *"Bring me a bottle of iced champagne, Monique, then instruct the pilot to get me the Russian President on the 'phone!"*

The apprehensive Stewardess, Monique, nodded and replied respectfully, *"Immediately, Your Excellency."*

Saddam had ensured that his personal aircraft was staffed with the best and most professional personnel and that it fitted out with the very finest, state of the art 'air to ground' communications equipment and that it always had access to SKY TV. Like everything else in his life, no expense had been spared. He sat back and waited to be connected to the Russian President, Baronovski.

Monique returned carrying the chilled champagne, the President's favourite, a bottle of Brunello Di Montalcino Reserve 1950 Biondi Santigh, (a snip at at £10,500 a bottle). He drank at least one bottle of the stuff a day.

Saddam also had an innate fondness for 'Tiger' beer which was flown in by the crate from Singapore for him, but had to keep a close eye on his consumption of it as he was starting to put on a little extra weight.

The Stewardess leant over and poured the sparkling champagne into an exquisite crystal champagne glass, not daring to spill a drop, and then carefully placed it on the table in front of Saddam, just as the small red light on the 'phone in front of him started to flash angrily.

"*Is there anything else that you require, Your Excellency?*" Monique asked. Saddam leered at her, licked his lips and said, "*Perhaps later, my dear,*" then waved her away.

Saddam picked up the telephone, took a sip of his champagne then said to his Russian counterpart, "*Mister President, how are you, my dear friend. I thought you'd like to know that I am now leaving Iraqi airspace and am on my way to Russia.*"

He listened, sipping his champagne, as the Russian President replied, "*I look forward to meeting you again, Saddam. You'll be delighted to know that all of the reception arrangements are well in hand. Have a safe journey and I will see you soon.*"

They both then broke the connection, keeping their calls necessarily short just in case they were being monitored by the 'enemy.'

On arrrival in Moscow, it was planned that Saddam would be met at the closed VIP airport by his dear friend, the Russian President himself, President Boris Baronovski, then be swept off under heavily armed guard to a pre-prepared huge and luxurious dacha where he would be reunited with key members of his own staff and family at a sumptuous, no expenses spared welcoming party.

Both of the Iraqi aircraft would then be unloaded of their passengers and precious cargo, then refuelled and flown out of Russia to Kazakhstan where arrangements had been made for them to be destroyed and their crews executed.

Having eyeballed Monique, Saddam had decided that the Stewardess would remain in Moscow for a few months, where she could cater for his every whim, after which, when boredom set in - as it inevitably did, Saddam would order that her services were to be dispensed with.

The Russian had arranged for Saddam's mistress, the glamorous Parisoula Lamapsos, to be provided with a secure luxury VIP apartment in central Moscow, hidden well away from the eyes of Saddam's fiery wife. The FSB had promised Saddam's Chief of Staff faithfully that never the twain would meet. The FSB could do the same for the Stewardess, Monique. Saddam's son Qusay would see to all of that.

It was taken as read that once Saddam had become bored with his mistress Parisoula, she would either be paid off or more than likely, like the unfortunate Stewardess, Monique, be disposed of, probably to a brothel. That particular suggestion from his son Qusay had amused Saddam no end. It appealed to his warped sense of humour.

Once he had settled in and got his breath back, Saddam would then begin making plans with his team, assisted by the Russians, for his eventual return to power in Iraq. After which, Saddam had sworn, he would make his enemies tremble and sweat with fear before they met their fate.

He was definitely not a man to be crossed. Saddam had a long memory and was an extremely cruel vindictive man who could be relied upon to exact a cruel revenge, no matter how long it took.

What Saddam was totally unaware of - and what Russian President Baronovski already knew, was that already things were beginning to fall apart for the ex-Iraqi President. Once Saddam arrived in Moscow he would be the recipient of some crushingly bad news.

Baronovski was dreading being the bearer of bad tidings regarding the demise of Saddam's two sons, Qusay and Uday and also his young nephew Mustapha, but he had to be told. Baronovski knew that Saddam's anger would be volcanic.

Ж

CHAPTER TWO

'SHOCK AND AWE'

It was the 22nd of July 2003 and a hot, dusty 'High Noon' in North East Mosul. American coalition forces had surrounded what was once a lavish but now heavily damaged, bullet chipped and marble splintered Mansion and were busy exchanging shots with the occupants of the building. The noise of weapons fire and grenades exploding was deafening. No-one dared move.

From behind a nearby shoulder-high garden wall within sight of the embattled Mansion, where they were both taking cover, local Iraqi shop owner Nabil turned to his neighbour Ahmed and said to him, *"So what is happening here then, my brother?"*

Ahmed replied, *"I am told that the Americans have cornered Qusay and Uday Hussein in the Mansion and are attempting to take them prisoner. From the sound of it though, the brothers are putting up quite a fight."*

'Brothers - Uday & Qusay Hussein'

"Allãhu akbar!" (God is Great!) said Nabil, *"At last those two murdering swine the Hussein's will get what's coming to them."* *"Oh, I don't know about that,"* said Ahmed, *"the fire-fight has been going on for quite some time now and the only ones to have suffered casualties seems have been the Americans. I witnessed several badly wounded American soldiers being evacuated from over there earlier."*

"How many of our brave Iraqi soldiers do the Hussein brothers have fighting alongside them?" asked Nabil. Ahmed shook his head, *"None, as far as I know. Although I heard someone saying that the President's Personal Secretary, Abid al-Hamid Mahmud and Qusay's 14 year old son Mustapha are in the building with the two brothers, but I don't know how true that is."*

'Lieutenant General Abid al-Hamid Mahmud'

"Are you telling me that just three men and a young boy are holding all of those Americans at bay?" asked Nabil. Ahmed nodded, *"Yes, and the four of them are fighting like demons, but they can't possibly hold out for much longer. They are cornered like rats in a trap."*

"What has happened to the repulsive owner of the Mansion and his slimy son, are they not also relatives of the President?" asked Nabil.

"Huh, those two! They were taken by the American earlier on this morning," said Ahmed. *"Alive?"* asked Nabil. *"Yes, alive and kicking!"* said Ahmed, *"I saw that with my own two eyes! Both father and son were arrested by the Americans when they arrived at the front door of the building, just before all the shooting began."*

"Did not the two of them put up a fight?" asked Nabil. *"No, they didn't raise a finger,"* replied Ahmed, *"they were both unarmed and came out of the building with their hands clasped to the backs of their necks!"*

Nabil looked confused, *"Surrendered, you mean?"* Ahmed nodded. *"But are they not both blood relatives of Saddam? Why did they not stick together and put up a fight?"* asked Nabil. Ahmed shook his head, *"Ask me a question on camel racing! I don't know the answer to that. That's what made me think that something unusual was going on. It puzzled me."*

"What do you mean, brother, something unusual?" asked Nabil.

Ahmed coughed, spat, then replied, *"Well, Saddam's two sons, his nephew and Abid al-Hamid Mahmud are upstairs in the building, battling like tigers for their lives, whilst those other two turds surrendered to the Americans without a fight. It is even rumoured that they were seen to be smiling as they were led away!"*

Nabil nodded and said, *"Call me old-fashioned, but I suppose it could be something to do with the 15 million dollar reward that has been placed on each of the Hussein brother's heads? What is that deck of cards thing that the Americans use to describe them?"*

"Uday is the 'Ace of Hearts' and Qusay is the 'Ace of Clubs,' said Ahmed, *"and we mustn't forget our beloved President?" "Oh him, he's the 'Ace of Spades' of course,"* said Ahmed.

"Well, he'll need a spade when they catch him. He'll be going six feet under!" said Nabil, flinching as another round of firing broke out over by the Mansion.

The US Defence Intelligence Agency had developed a set of playing cards to assist troops with identifying Saddam Hussein's high ranking members of the Arab Socialist Ba'ath Party, which included some of Saddam's family members. The playing cards were named 'Personality Identification Playing Cards.'

Ahmed nodded, *"You know, very little surprises me anymore, brother."* Nabil smiled, *"Huh, informers and blood money! Well, those two cowardly dogs who betrayed the Hussein's will be looking over their shoulders for the rest of their miserable lives. Saddam will not forgive or forget! He will eventually show them the sole of his shoe!"* he said.

As they were speaking, Americans reinforcements roared into the street in several dusty Humvees and drew to a halt just out of sight and line of fire of the Mansion. Things were obviously about to hot up. *"Is it not time we left here for a place of safety, my brother,"* said Nabil, *"things are about to kick-off and we don't want to get caught in the cross-fire."*

"I'm not moving from here, Nabil," replied Ahmed, *"we're far safer sheltering behind this wall for now. You know as well as I do that anything that moves now will be shot at either by the trigger-happy Americans or the lunatic Hussein's."*

Nabil nodded, *"Huh, some choice. Yes, you are, of course, correct."* He tutted, *"Just look at how many Americans there are arriving. There's definitely going to be a shit-storm!"*

The Major commanding the American troops already on the ground stepped over to one of the Humvees that had disgorged its occupants and spoke to the bird-colonel, who was stood there casually lighting a cigar. The Major saluted and introduced himself.

"Morning Colonel, I'm Major Mal E Kyng. I'm in command of the infantry here on the ground that initially tried to gain access to the Mansion where the Hussein's are hiding. I have orders from above to try and take them alive."

The Colonel nodded and returned a lazy salute, *"Morning Major, Colonel Silas Rushmore. By the way, that's enough saluting for today, eh!"* They shook hands. Nodding at the harassed Captain accompanying him, Colonel Rushmore introduced him, *"This is my Exec, Captain Johnny Wiles."* Johnny smiled and shook hands with the Major. *"OK, Mal,"* said Colonel Rushmore, *"can you gimme a quick sitrep re what's happening here."*

"Sure can, sir!" replied the Major.

"Well, Colonel, earlier today we got a call at base HQ informing us that Numbers Two and Three on the Central Command's Most Wanted List i.e. brothers Qusay and Uday Hussein, were known to be hiding inside that Mansion over there, along with Saddam Hussein's Personal Secretary, Abid al-Hamid Mahmud and Qusay's 14 year old son Mustapha."

The Colonel nodded, *"And?"*

Major Kyng continued, *"I was ordered to take an infantry platoon and hotfoot it over here and take the Hussein's and the others into custody. When I arrived here I gave them the opportunity to surrender, but they chose not to."*

"What did they say?" asked the Colonel. *"Nothing sir, I went across and shouted at them to surrender but they opened fire on us without any warning! That's when some of my guys got wounded."*

Colonel Rushmore said, *"Huh, OK. Well, I guess that we'd better get inside that building asap and give them a taste of their own medicine. Now I know that we've been ordered to take them alive, Mal, but between you and me, it'd be better to stiff them and save us the cost of a lengthy trial and why should we have to feed and water them for the next thirty years, eh!"* The Major nodded in agreement.

Rushmore continued, *"And there's a 14 year old kid in there with them, you say?"* Major Kyng nodded, *"Yes Colonel, Mustapha Hussein, son of Qusay Hussein."*

The Colonel nodded confidently, *"Well, you know what they say, Major. Little rats grow into big rats. We'd better get on inside that building and see what we can do about resolving this here little situation."*

Major Kyng continued, *"The owner of the Mansion and his son, distant cousins of Saddam Hussein, were taken into custody when we first arrived. They surrendered to us at the very beginning of the op. That part went well."*

"It was only when we entered the building, calling out for the others to surrender, then started to carry out the usual checks for trip-wires and booby traps that we came under heavy fire. Unfortunately, because those bastards opened

up on us without warning, some of our guys were hit, so I gave the order to withdraw."

"Yup, heard about that," said Colonel Rushmore, *"but I'm told that your boys are doing OK."* Major Kyng nodded, *"Yes, Colonel, we were lucky there - it could have been a lot worse!"*

"Yup, it don't pay to underestimate these crafty Ayrabs, Mal," (the Colonel pronounced it 'Ay-Rabs'). *"So why the hell is it taking so long to winkle them outta that building if there's only three men and a kid in there?"* asked the Colonel, nodding towards the Mansion.

"Don't be fooled by the building, Colonel. It might look like a bog-standard house, but it's more like a fortified bunker, sir. It's been built of reinforced concrete and the windows are made of bullet-proof glass, so they were well prepared," said Major Kyng.

"We scoped the building, Colonel, and saw that they'd moved up to the top floor. They've got the stairwell covered so that it's just a killing ground. I didn't want to take any more casualties so I withdrew and called for reinforcements."

The Colonel nodded, *"Wise move, Major. Would've done exactly the same myself. Well, we 'aint in any rush - and those guys up there sure as hell 'aint going no place - not on my watch anyway!"*

Looking across at the Mansion, Colonel Rushmore asked, *"I don't see much movement over there. Where abouts are they?"*

"Up on the far right corner of the top floor, sir, and that's where most of the incoming fire is coming from," replied Major Kyng, *"We made two further attempts to gain entry into the building, but we just can't get near them. The stairwell's the problem, it's literally an uphill battle."*

The Colonel nodded, *"Well Major, your guys took a bit of a kicking but we can deal with this, so let's get straight back on the horse and give 'em a spot of hot, eh!"*

The Colonel ducked as suddenly all hell broke loose when a heavy burst of shots was fired from the upstairs of the Mansion directly at the Americans, peppering their vehicles with rounds which sparked off the metal of the Humvees.

"Jeez, Mal, I see what ya mean!" said the Colonel, ducking, *"What the hell are they shooting at us with?"* he asked, *"Sounds like they're using AK-47's." "Yeah, AK-47's, Colonel,"* replied the Major.

Colonel Rushmore nodded, *"OK, then we're just gonna have to up our game a little bit, Mal! We're not taking any more shit from those rag-heads!"*

He turned to his Exec, *"Wilesy, get on the horn and send for the Cavalry!" "You got it, Colonel!"* replied the Exec, sprinting across to the command Humvee.

The Colonel, who was obviously enjoying himself, continued, *"In the meantime, Major, have some of your guys clear the Ayrab civilians away from the immediate area. When the 101st boys get here the odds are that the Mansion and probably some of those other buildings next to it will be trashed. Those 101st guys don't fanny about. They'll haul our irons out of the fire!"*

Major Kyng smiled, *"Aint that the truth, Colonel!"*

The Colonel tossed his cigar onto the floor and stomped on it with the heel of his boot, *"God damn these ceegars, they'll be the death of me,"* he said. *"Well, Mal, we've been instructed by the General to ensure that there'll be as few civilian casualties as possible in these here situations, 'Hearts and Minds' and all that sorta crap, huh, so we'd better go to it and move that crowd of Ayrab onlookers back!"*

Major Kyng nodded, *"OK Colonel, I'll get the guys straight on to it!"*

Not fifteen minutes later, reinforcements arrived in the shape of a hundred soldiers from 101st Airborne Division, bristling with weapons and accompanied by two fearsome OH-58D Kiowa Warrior helicopters. Things were about to go downhill rapidly for the unfortunate occupants of the Mansion.

'The OH-58D Kiowa Warrior Helicopter'

Peeking down from a cracked upstairs window of the Mansion, young Mustapha turned to his father Qusay and said, *"Father, look, American reinforcements have arrived and there's a lot of them!"*

Mustapha pointed nervously at the American vehicles and hovering helicopters, *"See, there are Humvees, helicopters and a lot more soldiers!"*

Qusay nodded and smiled. Ruffling his son's hair he said, *"Just keep your head down and don't worry my son, we are far from beaten yet. We will fight them and make our father, your beloved grandfather proud of us!"*

"Your father is right, nephew. We will take care of these American dogs," said Mustapha's Uncle Uday. *"then we will escape from here and make our way to the airport."*

No sooner had Uday spoken than all hell broke loose as the Americans suddenly opened fire with everything they had. The OH-58D Kiowa Warrior helicopters blasting off their 2.75-inch rockets, Mark-19 Grenade Launchers and AT-4 Rockets, supported by the Humvee-mounted fearsome .50 calibre machine-guns, chattering furiously as they sprayed the Mansion with lead from top to bottom. Huge chunks of masonry splintered off the walls and fell to the ground.

Despite the onslaught, the occupants of the Mansion fought determinedly on, returning fire as best they could. The noise went on for a few minutes, then suddenly all of the firing ceased and an eerie silence descended on the area, broken only by the occasional burst of chattering on the American's radios.

Hand on top of his helmet, Colonel Rushmore said to no-one in particular, *"Jeez, that was some kinda shit-storm, huh!"* Despite the power of the American attack, the occupants of the building had still managed to return heavy fire and hold them at bay.

Major Kyng said, *"See what I mean, Colonel. Those Hussein guys just don't know when to give in, huh!"* The Colonel turned to his Exec, *"Gimme a time check, will ya, Wilesy?"* His Exec replied, *"It's 1300 hours local, Colonel!"*

Rushmore said, *"Well, those mothers started this - but we'll sure as hell finish it. OK, Wilesy, go tell the 101 guys to loose off a couple of Tow's* (Ground Fired 10 Tube-launched Optically Tracked Wire-Guided Missiles) *and then pop some smoke!"*

He turned to Major Kyng and said, *"If that doesn't do the job I'll call for an AH-64 Apache helicopter or an Air*

Force A-10 Thunderbolt II. Either way, those camel jockeys sure aren't getting out of that building in one piece today!"

Rushmore's Exec nodded and radioed the instructions through to the ground troops. *"Let's give 'em a taste of American ordnance!"* said the Colonel, raising his rifle and loosing off a quick couple of rounds towards the Mansion himself.

"Jeez," thought Major Kyng, *"this crazy bastard thinks he's Arnie Schwarzenegger!"*

The Mansion remained strangely silent, the occupants not returning the Colonel's fire. *"They must be running out of ammo,"* said Colonel Rushmore.

'An American Humvee firing a TOW Missile'

At 1321 hours, several TOW's were fired directly at the Mansion, tearing through its reinforced walls and bullet proof windows as if they were rice paper, dispensing death and destruction to the occupants of the building.

Colonel Rushmore turned to Major Kyng and his Exec and said, *"That oughta do it,"* then ordered *"OK guys, better tell the men to 'Lock and Load' - let's go and finish this thing off!"*

Amazingly, and despite the severe damage to the upper floors of the Mansion, when the American soldiers made their way into the smoking and badly damaged building to mop up, they still came under fire from the top floor, although the rate of firing had been reduced to what sounded like just the one weapon.

"Easy does it, guys," said Major Kyng, leading from the front and stepping carefully over the mounds of rubble, *"Don't touch anything and keep an eye out for trip wires!"*

'The remains of the Mansion'

Remarkably, and despite the destruction unleashed by the TOW's, someone in the upper rooms had survived the American's fierce onslaught and was loosing off a few shots, although the rate of fire had been radically reduced.

Unfazed, the Americans charged heroically into the entrance of the building, ran up the stairs, 'hosing' the various rooms with rifle fire and spotted the one surviving attacker kneeling behind a bed in a corner of the top floor, surrounded by a mountain of empty shell cases.

The last opponent was struggling desperately to fit a fresh magazine to his red-hot weapon - whilst screaming obscenities in English at the Yanks. *"Splash him!"* shouted Major Kyng. Several of the Americans opened fire and silenced the last fighter.

The American soldiers discovered shortly afterwards that their final opponent, and the only survivor of the TOW onslaught, was the 14 year old Mustapha. The soldiers weren't too happy about it, but had no other option, it was kill or be killed.

'Mustapha Qusay Saddam al-Tikriti'

Major Kyng looked across at the shattered bullet ridden body of the 14 year old Mustapha, weapon still clutched in his lifeless hand and with several smoking and gaping holes across his chest.

The Major knelt down and lowering Mustapha's eye-lids, shook his head and said, *"Jeez, Colonel, he's just a kid. What a waste of a young life!"*

Stood behind Major Kyng, a totally unsympathetic Colonel Rushmore replied, *"That's the way the cookie crumbles, Mal. He got what he deserved, and anyway, he wouldn't have hesitated to drop you in your tracks. These Ayrabs just cain't take no for an answer!"* as he spoke he kicked Mustapha's weapon dispassionately out of the boys lifeless hands.

The upstairs room of what had once been a very glamorous Mansion now looked like a bombed out butcher's shop, with blood, gore and body parts splattered everywhere. *"Jesus H Christ, what a mess,"* thought Major Kyng.

Looking dispassionately around the shattered room, Colonel Rushmore ordered, *"OK, Mal, have these stiffs photographed, tagged and bagged, then we'd better get on outta here. The building looks as if it could collapse at any second,"* he glanced at his wristwatch, *"and anyway I don't know about you, but I'm feeling a little peckish. Time to tie on a nose-bag, huh!"*

A queasy Major King noted that the other occupants of the room, Abid al-Hamid Mahmud and brothers Uday and Qusay Hussein, had been shredded almost beyond recognition and that bits of their bodies were spread all around the room like parts of some obscene jig-saw. It was a grizzly scene.

Mal knew that with the exception of young Mustapha, who was still recognisable, it was going to be a difficult and time consuming task for the Medics to sort out and identify the remains of the other three men. Fortunately that wouldn't be his problem.

Colonel Rushmore, who was stood behind Major Kyng, casually lit up another cigar and said, *"Huh, don't feel any sympathy for those Hussein bastards, Mal. They've got more blood on their hands than we could ever imagine."*

The Colonel sucked on his glowing cigar, then theatrically blowing a smoke-ring out of his mouth, sighed, and said, *"What we gotta do now guys is find their Daddy, the 'Ace of Spades' and give him a taste of the same kinda medicine."* He turned to his Exec, *"Come on, Wilesy, time to saddle up and hit the trail! Gotta go - see ya back at the O.K. Corral, Mal!"*

The Colonel carelessly flicked his still burning cigar across the wrecked room and turned to leave. Major Kyng saluted Colonel Rushmore, *"Back at ya, Colonel. Probably bump into ya in the chow tent, sir."* The Colonel smiled, *"I'll get Wilesy here to save you a burger!"* he said as he stood on a piece of someone's mangled hand.

ЖК

CHAPTER THREE

'THE 'OP EXTRACTION' PLAN'

Mike Fraser and Graham St Anier were lounging in Mike's conference room, inside the offices of '*T2-Inc*' at Kingswood, near Hull, where Dutchman Ed De Jong was reaching the conclusion of a briefing regarding the plans for their forthcoming scheme to lift some of Saddam's dollars from the High Security Compound at Moscow's Sheremetyevo Airport.

For ease of reference, Ed had named the whole thing, '***OP EXTRACTION.***' Graham had cracked a joke about the name sounding like some sort of Dental Plan, which raised a titter. In view of what they were about to attempt, things were getting a little serious so a bit of a laugh didn't go amiss.

"So, in conclusion, my friends," said Ed*, " the plan is for us to enter the High Security Compound at Moscow's Sheremetyevo Airport, remove 26 pallets of the 200 or so that are stashed away there in a hangar and get the hell out of Moscow using my two URAL-4320 trucks."*

Ed pointed at a large map pinned to the wall and continued, *"We three will transport over to Moscow in the 'T3-Travellator' then dematerialise inside the compound. You'll see that I've deliberately timed the operation so that the two URAL-4320 cargo trucks, we call them 'Trumpeters' incidentally, will arrive there shortly after we do, after having been driven from Saint Petersburg to Moscow."*

"Now, guys, as we know from information received, each of the pallets inside the hangar contains $1 billion American dollars, money that's been stored there supposedly on behalf of Saddam Hussein - despite Russian denials to the contrary."

"Our aim is to get some 26 of the pallets out of there and truck them to Saint Petersburg in the two URAL's, after which the money will transferred into metal cargo containers ready to be shipped across to Rotterdam via Helsinki."

"On arrival in the Port of Rotterdam, the containers will then be craned off the ship by my guys and trucked safely back to my security compound in Amsterdam. That's how I propose we do it."

Graham interrupted him. *"Excuse me butting in, Ed, I'm not being greedy, but why only 26 pallets and not more?"* he asked. *"More manageable, my friend. I prefer to keep it down to two truck loads. I'll explain why in a moment,"* said Ed. Graham nodded.

Ed continued, *"Each of those pallets in the compound is stacked with a billion crisp American dollars, money that rightfully belongs to the people of Iraq. I've given the amount we can carry a great deal of thought and think that its safer and easier to keep to just the two truck loads. That's why I planned for the removal of only 26 pallets; I know that 13 pallets will fit nicely onto each truck."*

"Basically, I already have two trucks and two drivers that I regularly use on delivery/collection runs from the Russian Port of Saint Petersburg down to the Moscow area as part of my other 'business' interests. My two boys, Deiderick and Ludo, have agreed to accompany the trucks. So, everything dove-tails in nicely."

"Once we've loaded our trucks with the dollar-laden pallets, the vehicles and crews will clear off out of the compound at Shermeteyov Airport, and head on up the road for Saint Petersburg. We three will get back on-board the 'T3-Travellator' and zoom off to Amsterdam."

"That, gentlemen, is just a simplified and broad overview of the operation. The specific plan is rather more complex, but I have every confidence that it will succeed."

"Also, I would like you to consider this. I think that some of the money, in all fairness, should be re-distributed once we've got it safely out of Russia. What I propose is that the rightful owners, the Iraqi's, should get something in the region of $20 billion, the Brits and Americans $2 billion each, and our little 'T-2' organisation will retain

the $2 billion balance - for services rendered. After all, there's more than enough to go around."

"That seems fair enough as far as the Iraqis are concerned, and I'm not being greedy, Ed, but why give the Brits and the Yanks anything?" queried a puzzled Graham.

Ed replied, *"In essence, the Brit and Yank's payments will both act as 'sweeteners.' The Brits - firstly under the guise of war reparations and also to ensure that they'll grant us an official license to 'Time-Travel' and use the 'T3-Travellator' to enter the compound in Moscow."* "Fair enough," said Graham, "And the Yanks?"

Ed continued, *"The Yanks get their $2 billion as compensation towards the money they expended getting rid of Saddam Hussein, and also for giving us access to their security contacts in Moscow, if needed, in the event of an emergency."*

"In the unlikely event of things going 'tits-up' - as Graham would say, we might need to call upon either the Brit or the American undercover security service agents in Moscow for help. I have contacts in both organisations and know how to get in touch with them quickly if required."

Mike looked across at Graham and said, *"I'm more than happy with that so far. How about you Graham?"* Graham nodded, *"Sound as a pound. Crack on, Ed, I'm intrigued."*

"OK guys." continued Ed, *"I'm sure that you're wondering just how we are going to achieve the successful removal of those rather cumbersome dollar laden pallets from the closely guarded Russian Security Compound?"*

Mike and Graham nodded in unison.

"Well, for that particular segment of the robbery," said Ed, *"which, as you know, I have entitled, perhaps a little theatrically,* **'OPERATION EXTRACTION'**' *I plan to use my two beefy and very reliable Russian URAL-4320 'Trumpeters' to transport the pallets."*

'A URAL-4320 Trumpeter'

"I already have the vehicles in my possession and have used the 'Trumpeters' frequently for various forays to and from 'Mother Russia,' although I have made sure that they are not traceable back to me.

I will also be using two of my best drivers throughout the operation, Artyom Bogdanovitch and Kostya Liochka. Kostya, by the way, is a female." Graham smiled, nudged Mike and winked, *"Things are looking up, Mike,"* said Graham.

A smiling Ed continued, *"Don't get fired up, Graham. Kostya is built like a brick shit-house and could easily eat you for breakfast! Anyway, Kostya and Artyom are an item. They've both worked for me for several years on various er, shall we say, commercial enterprises. A very professional team, they're extremely reliable and more importantly - trustworthy. We've been doing profitable 'business' happily together for very many years."*

"As you guys both know, I don't actually need the money that my smuggling activities brings in; it's more of a 'hobby' for me, but I do it because I like to 'cock a snook' at the Russian Border Service every now and again. Keeps them on their toes."

"Now, on this operation my two sons Ludo and Deiderick will accompany the trucks from Saint Petersburg to Moscow, acting as 'co-pilots.' They will remain with the vehicles and money throughout the majority of the extraction operation, up to and including returning to the docks at Saint Petersburg, then on to the Port of Rotterdam, via Helsinki."

"Once the money is on its way from the compound, we three will then simply jump back onboard the 'T3' and return home. Oh, and as a side issue, it will also be necessary for us to bring my Russian contact from the compound with us. For obvious reasons it will unsafe for that person to remain there after the robbery."

Ed smiled, *"Now, I have it on good authority, er, money and duty-free goods changed hands, that inside the*

Russian Security Compound at the Sheremetyevo Airport, there is an FD30 3 Ton Petrol Forklift with a most reliable Isuzu engine. We can use it to cross-load the 26 dummy pallets being taken there by our cargo vehicles, in readiness to replace them with the real dollar-laden ones."

"Both of our truck drivers are familiar with that model of forklift, but just to be on the safe side I'll hire a similar one so that they can practise using it to load and unload their trucks with similar sized pallets. That will also give us an idea of how long it will take to swop the dud pallets over with the dollar laden ones."

"Och, I'm liking this!" said Mike.

Ed smiled and continued, *"Naturally we have to allow for such things as the Russian Security Services arriving unannounced to do spot checks on the compound, although my informant tell me that currently they are more than a little slack in that particular area. Time, though, will be of the essence. We will need to be slick and get in and out of that compound as quickly as we can. Every second counts."*

"You will have realised by now that I have a contact working inside the Sheremetyevo Airport Security Compound who has agreed to meet up with us in situ to guide us around, once we have agreed upon a date and time for the raid to take place. My contact has also agreed to provide us with all of the important minutiae relating

to guard strengths, procedures, patrol timings, security inspections etc."

"*Good Lord, you have been a busy wee goose, Ed. So precisely where do we three fit into the grand plan then?"* asked Mike. *"I was just coming on to that, Mike,"* said Ed.

"*Basically, the idea is that we three will dematerialise inside the compound in the 'T3-Travellator' where my contact will be waiting for us and then we can prepare the ground for the arrival of my two trucks. The trucks will be arriving at the main gate of the compound just after it gets dark. My contact will arrange for them to be given immediate access to the site."*

"*The fully-fuelled trucks will arrive carrying dummy pallets that mirror exactly the shape, size and wrappings of the dollar laden pallets that we are going to exchange them for. We will then simply cross-load the pallets on a 'one-for-one' basis. My trucks are fitted with side curtains which will make the process relatively straightforward. So, it's simply a matter of one off, one on."*

"*The cross-loading needs to be completed by no later than midnight, by which time our trucks must be out of that compound like shit off a shovel and heading away from Moscow, and on their way back to Saint Petersburg whilst it's dark and the roads are relatively quiet."*

"At Saint Petersburg the pallets will then be loaded into 20 foot steel cargo containers, ready for transferring to a cargo ship, which will be sailing to Helsinki."

"At Helsinki the cargo containers will be transferred to another ship, which will then head for the Port of Rotterdam - where we will be waiting to collect them."

"Once the URAL-4320's and their crews have left the Russian compound, we three and the Russian 'Deep Throat' will then jump on board the 'T3-Travellator' and Time-Transport ourselves over to the Netherlands."

"After the cargo containers have arrived at the Port of Rotterdam we'll transfer them to my high security compound in Amsterdam. Before you ask, we don't have to concern ourselves with the Customs and Excise procedures at Rotterdam. That aspect has already been well taken care of." Mike and Graham smiled knowingly.

Ed continued, "The route leaving Moscow via the Leningrad Highway can be a little complicated, but the two truck drivers, Artyom and Kostya, have driven the route many times and know exactly which roads to take, which 'poo traps' to avoid and which palms to cross along the way, if required. The distance from Moscow to Saint Petersburg, using the M10 Motorway, is approximately 700 kilometres."

"Hell fire, 700 kilometres, that's a bit of a flog," said Graham. Ed nodded, "That's precisely why we need two solid, reliable trucks and two good drivers."

Pointing at the wall map, Ed continued, *"The route runs through, or goes very near to places that you've probably never heard of, like Khimini, Tver, Vyshny, Veliky Novgorod, Chudov and Tosno, where there are refuelling and stop-off points should we need them, which in theory we shouldn't. Our trucks will be carrying sufficient spare jerricans of fuel so that we don't have to hang about. Kostya and Artyom will have their pedals to the metal!"*

"A few 'factoids.' The motorway peters out at the city border of Saint Petersburg in the Pushinsky district. On arrival there, the trucks will be driven straight to an industrial area near the docks where there's a secure freight yard owned by a very close friend of mine. The trucks can then be tucked out of sight and unloaded, away from prying eyes."

"The contents of the pallets will be loaded inside two bog standard twenty foot Hapag-Lloyd shipping cargo containers, which will then be sealed and ferried to the docks to be craned onboard the Finnlandlines cargo freighter, the 'MV Solar Star.'"

"The 'Trumpeter' trucks will then be completely dismantled and the various parts 'deep-sixed.' There must be no evidence whatsoever left of them for the Russian FSB to find. Anyway, the trucks will have outlived their usefulness and must disappear from the face of the earth. Similarly, the drivers, Artyom and Kostya, will vanish into the mist. I've promised them that as a result of this run they'll both make enough money to retire."

"My two boys, Deiderick and Ludi will not accompany the 'MV Solar Star' from Saint Petersburg but will travel by road, as tourists, along the 'Scandinavian Highway' from Saint Petersburg to the Finnish Border, a distance of about 210 km, then they'll jump on board a train and travel through to Helsinki. I want them both to be well out of Russia so that they can't be associated with any of this. The last thing I want is for them to be hauled in by the FSB."

"On arrival at Helsinki my lads will jump on board the 'MV Europe Oceana' a different 'Finnlandlines' cargo ship to the one that will arrive carrying our two cargo containers. The 'MV Europe Oceana' takes a few paying passengers as well as cargo; we have used the shipping line many times and they're very discreet."

"By the time the lads arrive on board the 'MV Europe Oceana,' our cargo containers will have been transferred from the 'MV Solar Star' and then my boys can keep an eye on the loot right through to the Port of Rotterdam where it will be unloaded and driven off to my compound in Amsterdam."

Ed smiled, *"As usual, palms will have to be crossed at each key stage of the journey, but with the amount of money that we are monkeying around with - I don't envisage that being a problem."*

"Now, gentlemen, I have given you both a fairly long but very simplified overview of the **'OP EXTRACTION'** *plan, the complete plan is obviously a lot more complex*

and detailed. The whole thing will be dangerous because at any time during the robbery we could be discovered by the Russian authorities and all hell will break loose."

"Once they find out what's happened, you can guarantee that our friends in the Russian FSB will be out in force searching for us. I am relying on the fact that we'll be long gone from the area before the loss is reported and they have the roads, railways, canals and everything else sealed off."

"It will be a risky enterprise. Not only will we have to contend with anything that the FSB may care to throw at us, but we'll also have to watch out for the Border Service of the Federal Security Service of the Russian Federation - which has some 170,000 members, including the Russian Maritime Border Guard Units - and let me assure you that they are all very professional."

"Bloody hell," said Graham, *"with all that lot snapping at our heels, it'll be like something from World War 2. All that'll be missing will be a few thousand White Russians chasing after us on horseback!"*

Mike grinned, *"Aye, it'll definitely be like World War 2 when the wee man President Baronovski himself finds out that we've nicked $26 billion dollars that he's supposed to be taking care of. Heads and Deputy Heads will definitely roll!"*

"The operation sounds a bit complex," said Ed, *"but I'm confident that we can pull this off, guys. It's no more*

difficult than any of the other stuff that we've done before."

"Over the past few years I personally have been involved with various organisations, in a business capacity, in that 'iffy' neck of the woods and have established many reliable contacts. We shouldn't have too many problems, once we've got the two trucks loaded, rolling out of the compound and away from the immediate danger zone, Moscow."

"It'll be expensive setting all of this up to get the money out of Moscow and safely away from the Russian authorities," said Ed, *"but when we are dealing in such astronomically profitable amounts, then money really is no object to us – and think of the fun we'll have lifting it!"*

Mike laughed and said, airily, *"Aye, and we can well afford to be generous with other people's money."* Graham chipped in, *"Careful Mike, you're beginning to think and sound like a Yorkshireman!"*

Ed looked at Graham and Mike, *"So, any comments or questions on what I've outlined so far, gentlemen?"*

"It all sounds perfectly straightforward to me," said Mike, *"you've obviously given this matter a great deal of thought - and there's tons of planning gone into it. Aye, it's going to be a wee bit of a challenge, but speaking for myself, I cannae wait tae get stuck in!"*

"Yes, I've been burning a great deal of midnight oil and of course it won't be particularly straightforward, there's always an element of the unexpected" replied Ed, "but don't forget, my friends, that I have a great deal of experience with these matters. Indeed, I have been making a very good living out of mischief for many years."

They all laughed.

"On a more serious note, unfortunately the Border Service of the Federal Security Service of the Russian Federation seems to be getting rather more probing these days and they've been getting uncomfortably close to uncovering some of my more profitable activities for some time. I think that this had better be my last bit of 'business' in Mother Russia for the moment."

Graham nodded, "Better to be safe than sorry, Ed. You know what'll happen if they get their hands on you!" Ed nodded. "I know, and I've had a few close calls let me tell you."

Ed stretched, then continued, "Now guys, if you could take a glance at those two files in front of you, one of which contains the financial considerations and the other the complete operational planning details, you will see that I have worked out a preliminary costing and made a good start on the 'plan of attack.' We can tweak it where necessary."

"Initially we're going to have to let our off-shore accounts take the financial strain in order to get our operation up *and running. I'm assuming that you have no problem with that particular aspect, chaps?"* asked Ed.

"*Easy come, easy go,*" said a smiling Mike. "*Speculate to accumulate!*" said Graham. "*Great,*" said Ed, "*well, we'd better crack on with the pre-planning then.*" "*I'm gagged, let me put the kettle on first,*" said Mike.

"*You know what, lads, I'm starting to get really fired up with this one. I was beginning to get a bit stale just sat at home all day gazing at the telly,*" said Graham, "*I've watched so many bloody cookery programmes that I'm nearly qualified to be a cordon bleu chef and anyway the telly's not been the same since they took the Jeremy Kyle Show off air!*"

"*If we pull this particular blagging off successfully, you'll be able to employ your own cordon bleu chef,*" said Ed.

Ж

CHAPTER FOUR

'THE COMPOUND'

Although it was a typically dismal Russian day and one, to use an old naval phrase, that would certainly freeze the balls off a brass monkey, Captain Rostislav Anatoly Zoranski was perspiring profusely, (or *'sweating chuffing cobs'* as Graham would have put it).

The Captain, an out of condition, gouty, borderline alcoholic, was only a few years away from retirement, (that's if his liver didn't give up the ghost before he did). Like his now shoddy uniform, Zoranski had seen better days.

His current post was 2IC (Second-in-Command) of the armed guard at Moscow's Sheremetyevo Airport's High Security Compound. The Compound was tucked away out of sight, well inside the airport. Zoranski's job, was to be his final military assignment before being put out to grass.

Zoranski was dreading the day when his regular military income would stop and then he'd have to eke out an existence on a very small army pension. He had no substantial savings to fall back on and would, he knew, have to live hand to mouth. It wasn't something that he was looking forward to with great relish.

To date, Captain Zoranski's military career had been spectacularly unsuccessful, primarily because of his over-consumption of alcohol, a result of which was that he'd been side-lined to low-grade, non-taxing posts for many years. Even then, he had often been on the cusp of being sacked.

Early on in his career, a previous Commanding Officer of his had written on one of Zoranski's annual confidential reports, *"Not only has this officer reached his ceiling - he has put his head through it!"* For Zoranski that one comment alone was a career show-stopper.

The one and only reason that Captain Zoranski had been posted to Moscow, considered by some to be a plum posting, and not to some long forgotten outpost in the Far East, was that he originated from the city.

Unusually, someone in the military records office decided to do him a favour by tucking him out of sight at the Sheremetyevo High Security Compound, thinking that it would help him at the conclusion of his military service, when his time came to resettle in the area.

The dissolute Captain Rostislav Anatoly Zoranski was Ed De Jong's 'inside man' at the High Security Compound.

Realising at the pre-planning stage of the robbery that he'd have to establish contact with someone who had an inside knowledge of the Security Compound and its workings, Ed De Jong had contacted a long-time friend of his for help. The man, Boris 'The Scorpion' Krensky, was someone who had been a part of Ed's previous existence in the shadowy life of Special Forces was now enjoying himself wallowing in luxury being the head of one of Moscow's top crime syndicates.

An experienced Special Forces man, Ed had worked alongside Israel's Sayeret Matkal, France's National Gendarmerie Group, Spain's Unidad de Operaciones Especiales, Pakistan's 'Black Storks - the Special Services Group - and even at one stage alongside the Russian's Alpha Group, which is where he'd crossed paths with 'The Scorpion.' They became friends for life.

Krensky, now out of the security forces and an 'entrepreneur' who owned several nightclubs, brothels and casinos, was referred to throughout the Russian underworld as 'The Scorpion' simply because he'd had a fearsome looking scorpion tattooed on the side of his neck when he was a young man.

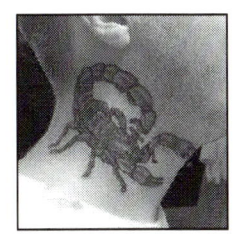

It was a tattoo of which Boris was inordinately proud, particularly as, he often boasted, it had been done without any form of anaesthetic, the tattooist using a large darning needle attached to an old fashioned electric shaver and several colours of bottled ink, now faded. He could easily have had the tattoo removed but had chosen not to do so. He felt that it added to his air of mystique.

During the course of his shadowy career and whilst participating in a joint British SAS covert operation in Afghanistan, Ed had bumped into and made friends with Scotsman Mike Fraser. Like Mike, Ed was a hard case who didn't suffer fools gladly; he was definitely not someone to be taken for granted.

If Ed liked and trusted you then he was a friend for life. If he didn't, then it was better to keep well out of his way, unless you wanted to risk having your 'lips ripped,' one of Ed's favourite phrases.

Ed liked and trusted Mike Fraser implicitly, he also liked and trusted Boris 'The Scorpion' Krensky - after all, they shared similar shady backgrounds. They knew that when they had their backs to the wall, they could count on each other for help. Over the years and in various 'hot spots' they'd had their backs to the wall on more than one occasion.

Ed decided to approach 'The Scorpion' for help. After a surreptitious bit of sniffing around and pulling in a few favours, Krensky had come up with the name of a Russian officer, Captain Rostislav Anatoly Zoranski, and passed it on to Ed - no questions asked.

'The Scorpion' had informed Ed that the Russian Captain was known to be someone who was openly susceptible to bribery and corruption, particularly after he'd been hitting the bottle, which was usually on most days.

Captain Zoranski could and would happily sell fuel, rations, military equipment and the like - just so long as you 'crossed his palm with silver.' Zoranski was also not averse to dipping his sticky fingers firmly into the military till and had several soldiers who had never existed written into the unit pay-roll, pocketing their salaries.

Such was the size and complexity of Russia's military administrative beaurocracy, that luckily for Zoranski he hadn't been caught - yet, but it was inevitable that some snoop would discover exactly what he'd been up to and he would then be court martialled. It was only a matter of time. The Captain trod a very thin line on a daily basis. Because of the pressure, he drank to forget, but had been drinking for so long that he couldn't really remember why he'd started in the first place.

Ed had made arrangements with 'The Scorpion' for him to 'coincidentally' bump into Zoranski at one of the several rather sleazy Moscow gambling dens/nightclubs that 'The Scorpion' owned and ran with an iron fist.

Zoranski frequented one such establishment, the 'Mon Cherie,' nightclub, the design of which 'The Scorpion' had based upon Berlin's infamous Charlottenburg 'Grotty Charlotty' nightclub, where as a younger man 'The Scorpion' had spent many happy hours and had become well known for being a big spender, making him extremely popular with the hostesses.

The Moscow version of 'Mon Cherie' was where most of Zoranski's money was frittered away on blowsy women and drinking copious amounts of nondescript fizzy German Sekt, re-bottled and disguised as quality French champagne.

Eventually, after 'worming' his way into Zoranski's confidence by buying him plenty of booze and making friends with him, Ed had gained his trust and offered the Captain what was to him an incredible and life-changing amount of money as a bribe to become 'Team Ed's' 'Deep Throat' for the planned robbery of the High Security Compound.

The clincher was Ed promising Captain Zoranski that immediately after the robbery, of which he would have an equal share in the proceedings, that he'd arrange to have him smuggled safely out of Russia , probably to Canada – furnished with a new identity, a new counterfeit passport and supporting documents such as a driving licence.

Once in Canada, Zoranski could then easily drop out of sight and more than likely would, using his newly acquired wealth and protected by a new identity, proceed to live the 'Life of Riley' and inevitably drink himself into an early grave.

Recognising that it was, for him, a seminal moment, Zoranski had accepted Ed's offer as quickly as a drowning man grabs a lifebelt. For Zoranski it was a no-brainer, the pension for a retired Captain in the Russian Army was a relative pittance, especially when compared with the mind-blowing sum of money that Ed was offering him.

It hadn't taken Zoranski long to work out that he'd be able to spend the remainder of his days in unimaginable luxury. To him it was better than a much dreamed of state lottery win.

As far as Captain Zoranski was concerned, he had very little to lose and everything to gain, so without further ado he'd volunteered his services. He'd long since realised that his military pension would hardly keep him in cheap vodka and not only that, the strain of him being caught fiddling military funds had become almost unbearable!

Zoranski knew that Ed's generous offer would provide him with the one and only opportunity to get away scot-free from his current miserable existence and spend his remaining years in relative comfort. He might even be able to find himself a decent woman.

So, for Zoranski, as Ed had counted on, the decision was straightforward. It was a 'Win-Win' situation for both of them.

Ed had explained to Zoranski that on the day of the robbery, a machine called a 'T3-Travellator' would 'dematerialise' in a quiet corner of the compound and disgorge its three occupants, of which Ed would be one.

The three of them and Zoranski would then wait for the arrival of Ed's two trucks and that's when the 'extraction' segment of the operation could begin.

The Captain was unable to fully understand the conceptual element of 'Time-Travel' a vital part of the operation, despite having had it explained to him several times by a very patient Ed.

The principle of 'Time-Travel' using a 'T3-Travellator' had gone straight over Captain Zoranski's head Nevertheless, after Ed had explained his outline 'robbery' plan, Zoranski had decided to put his faith in both the 'T3' and 'Team Ed.'

Zoranski wasn't particularly concerned about precisely how the robbery was going to take place, he just wanted to know when he'd receive his share and how he'd be spirited away from Russia in one piece once the robbery had been carried out.

Ed had warned Mike and Graham that he thought the Russian Captain was '*as thick as two lavatory seats*' but assured them that Zoranski's greed, desperation and avarice had quickly and easily subsumed his military responsibilities and loyalties.

Zoranski was champing at the bit and raring to go.

'Team Ed' agreed that they had no option but to rely on Zoranski's assistance to get them into the compound and look after them for the few hours that they were inside there, helping themselves to a vast quantity of Saddam Hussein's American dollars. Zoranski was their one and only chance.

Ж

CHAPTER FIVE

'BREAKING AND ENTERING'

A nervous Captain Zoranski was pacing around the inside of the High Security Compound at Sheremetyevo Airport, filled with equal amounts of vodka and trepidation, awaiting the arrival of the 'T3-Travellator.' After a very long day and one that seemed to drag on for an eternity, the moment had finally arrived for **'OPERATION EXTRACTION'** to swing into action.

Zoranski glanced at his cheap wrist watch and thought of the whimsical little saying, "*Time flies like an arrow, fruit flies like a banana!*" He was fully committed to his part in the forthcoming robbery and understood that once the 'T3-Travellator' arrived in the compound, if it did, then for him there would be no going back.

Despite reducing his overall intake, Zoranski had been knocking back vodka for the best part of the afternoon. The amount that he'd swallowed would have stunned a Holstein-Friesian bullock, but apart from his speech being slightly slurred it appeared not to have had any detrimental effect on him. He was a well-seasoned drinker.

Recognising the by now familiar symptoms, the glazed eyes, the slurred speech, the Russian compound guards steered well clear of Zoranski. He was also known for being bad-tempered, becoming both grouchy and unapproachable, particularly during the late afternoons as he slugged his way towards the bottom of yet another bottle of vodka.

Because Zoranski regularly sat in his office, usually in an alcohol induced depressed world of his own, the compound guards took advantage of that and were relatively slack in carrying out their guard duties. After all, Zoranski hardly ever left his office to check up on them, so why should this particular day be any different?

If only they'd known what was about to happen they might not have been quite so complacent.

So far, though, it had been a very quiet and normal day. The 'phone in the guardroom had rung only infrequently and apart from the expected radio checks every couple of hours, the radio connecting them to their Command Headquarters had remained blissfully silent.

The OC (Officer Commanding) placed in overall charge of the High Security Compound at Sheremetyevo, a louche and passed-over Major, Major Leonid Viktor Orlov, whose office was situated several kilometres away from the compound, hardly ever visited there and delegated everything to Zoranski. Almost all of the two's liaison duties were conducted over the 'phone and they very rarely met.

Throughout its entire existence, there had never been a breach in the compound's security and it was thought highly unlikely that there ever would be. After all, where could be safer than a High Security Compound tucked away inside a closely monitored Moscow airport and where the inner fenced-off area of that compound was patrolled 24 hours a day by armed guards? Only a fool would need to concern himself about something so blatantly safe.

The compound was considered by all and sundry as being as *"Secure as the inside of the Kremlin!"*

Considering what was about to happen, Major Orlov would have to write *"Secure as the inside of the Kremlin,"* in his 'book of famous last words' - if, that was, the FSB permitted him to retain enough fingers to write with, should he ever have the misfortune to experience their 'care and custody' package.

Peering through reddened, bleary eyes, Zoranski peered at his battered old wrist-watch and mumbled to himself, *"If it's going to happen, it will happen any moment now."* Then, suddenly, as if prompted, over in a darkened corner of the compound and immediately adjacent to the hangar where the money was located, a movement caught his eye and the 'T3-Travellator' de-materialised, exactly as Ed had described.

Zoranski's jaw dropped in surprise. So, what the Dutchman had explained to him about 'Time-Travel' was patently true. It was unbelievable.

It was exactly as the Dutchman had described, one minute there was absolutely nothing to see there, the next - in the gloom of the compound stood the Dutchman's 'Time-Machine' the 'T3-Travellator' - having arrived completely unnoticed by anyone else and with hardly any noise whatsoever. *"What will they think of next?"* thought Zoranski.

Striding across to the 'T-3 Travellator,' the apprehensive Zoranski realised that there would be no going back now, he was fully committed and was in it right up to his neck.

He recalled that many moons ago when he was a young officer cadet undergoing basic training, he'd been asked by an Instructor, *"Officer Cadet Zoranski - what's the difference between a pig and a chicken in a bacon and egg breakfast?"*

After shaking his head and looking more confused than he normally did, Zoranski had been told by the frustrated Instructor that, *"The chicken was involved but the pig was committed."* Like the doomed pig, Zoranski was now committed.

As the Captain reached the 'T-3 Travellator' he skidded to a halt just as a concealed door in its side hissed open, startling him. To Zoranski's great relief, a relaxed and smiling Ed De Jong stepped out. Ed said, *"Ah, good evening, Captain Zoranski. Great to see you!"* A relieved Zoranski returned Ed's smile and they shook hands.

"*Permit me to introduce my two partners in crime, Graham St Anier and Mike Fraser,*" said Ed, as his two companions stepped out of the 'T3.' "*What strange unpronounceable names these foreigners have,*" thought Rostislav Anatoly Zoranski, as he shook hands with Mike and Graham.

"*Hello, my dear fellow,*" said Mike, followed by a hearty "*Na then, old cock!*" and friendly wink from Graham.

"*Right, well that's the niceties out of the way, so we'd better get a move on, my friends,*" said Ed, looking at his watch, "*our two cargo trucks will be arriving here very shortly and we must be ready to receive them.*"

Zoranski nodded, "*Not to worry, Ed, everything is in hand; I have given precise instructions to my soldiers. They are under the impression that there is about to be a legitimate 'snap' security inspection of the compound.*"

"*I have ordered them to let the so-called 'inspection team' into the compound immediately, without any of the usual checks, then the guards are to keep themselves out of the way in the guardroom for the duration of the 'inspection' or until I personally stand them down.*"

"*The armed guards at the main gate, whom I should tell you do not have Field Marshal's batons in their rucksacks, are not the brightest of men and will let your vehicles inside here immediately they arrive and without going through the normal security procedures. They will then secure the compound gates behind them. After that, I will handle everything."*

Zoranski, sounded much more confident than he felt.

Ed nodded and asked, *"And the hangar containing the dollars?"*

Zoranski turned and pointed to one of the two hangars, *"You are standing right outside it. It's a secure building, so I've got the access code for the electronic security keypad there on the wall, which will allow us to gain immediate entry. Once the hangar doors slide open we can move the trucks and your 'Time-Machine' straight inside and get them hidden out of sight,"* said Zoranski, *"The hangar doors themselves are electrically operated, so will not pose us a problem."*

"Electronic doors eh," said Mike, *"No expense spared here boys!"* Zoranski shrugged his shoulders, *" Huh, those hangar doors are about the only things that work efficiently in this compound!"*

Ed turned to Graham, *"G, can you transport the 'T-3' inside the hangar and tuck it away out of sight whilst the Captain is opening the hangar doors?"* Graham nodded, *"No prob. Mike and I will go and sort that out. Come on Mike!"* They both headed off to the Travellator.

In the distance, the growling of truck engines could be heard in the distance as they drove up towards the compound, shortly after which Ed's two chunky Russian

URAL-4320 Cargo Trucks came into view, drawing to a halt at the main entrance gate of the compound. The driver of the front vehicle flashed the truck's headlights and tooted the horn.

Two Russian armed guards stepped smartly forward, opened the gates then raised the barrier and waved the trucks straight through as they'd been instructed to do by Captain Zoranski.

The trucks then rolled slowly across the tarmac to where Captain Zoranski and his visitors were standing, then drew to a halt.

The passenger door of the first truck swung open and Ed's son, Deiderick, jumped out. He ran across and gave his father a hug, saying, *"Hi Pops, sorry we're a bit late. There's a hell of a lot of military traffic about on the outskirts of Moscow tonight, so we took things easy so as not to raise any suspicions. We did OK timing wise though, just a few minutes late, eh!"*

Ed nodded, *"Better to be safe than sorry, Deiderick. Well done, son."* He glanced at his wristwatch, *"We're still doing OK for time though."*

"Now," Ed continued, *"our good friend Captain Zoranski here will show you where the trucks need to go, so let's get straight on with it. The sooner we're loaded up and out of here, the better. Just follow his instructions."*

Diedrick reached across and shook hands with Captain Zoranskik, "*Captain.*" Zoranski nodded and gave a nervous smile.

Zoranski turned and pointed towards the hangar, "*I will go and open those hangar doors, then your trucks and the 'Time-Machine' can be taken inside. I will then close the hangar doors, so remind your drivers to switch their engines off immediately they get inside, please. The fumes!*"

Deiderick nodded and returned to the trucks to give the drivers their instructions.

Captain Zoranski strode across to the nearby hangar and with trembling, cold fingers, lifted up the lid of a hinged metal box on the wall containing a wall-mounted electronic security key pad, then carefully tapped in the access code.

After a few heart-stopping seconds the large metal hangar doors started to rumble open on well-greased wheels. Several huge orange sodium lights in the hangar switched on automatically, which as they warmed up gradually increasing in brightness until the inside of the hangar was bathed in light.

Ed's two truck drivers, Artyom and Kostya carefully manoeuvered their large vehicles inside the now well lit hangar, parked up and then switched the truck's rumbling engines off, as per Zoranski's instruction.

By that time, Graham and Mike had jumped back inside the 'T-3' and a few moments later it had disappeared only to dematerialise inside a corner of the hangar.

Stepping out of the 'T-3' Graham said, *"There you are, old lad, not a bad bit of navigating, eh. And, might I add, only a few feet out from where we arrived in the compound!"*

"Aye, you've earned yourself a gold star, but that's only because you had the expert assistance of a very professional co-pilot, i.e. me!" said Mike.

Ed, followed Zoranski into the hangar, where Zoranski then repeated the procedure of tapping the numeric code into an inner wall-mounted electronic security key pad, and the hangar doors swiftly closed, sealing them all safely inside.

Zoranski had known that in his regularly innebriated state he might not have been able to remember the correct sequence of access numbers for the hangar's electronic security key pads, so he'd written them in pencil on his grubby shirt cuff.

In the 'heat of battle' he'd forgotten that he'd done that and had wiped his cuff across his sweaty forehead. Luckily the sweat had had very little effect on the pencil marks which were, fortunately, still legible.

How easily everything could have fallen at the first hurdle.

"*Right,*" said Ed, "*Deiderick, you and Ludo go and get the side panels of the trucks rolled up, then see if their fuel tanks need topping up, whilst Artyom and Kostya get cracking with the forklift. Mike, if you and Graham could go and check that the pallets are loaded with American dollars, please.*"

Mike and Graham nodded and hot-footed it across to the centre of the hangar to examine the contents of the pallets. "*It'd be a bit of a show-stopper of the pallets were empty and not hooching with dollars!*" Mike said to Graham. "*They'll be there all right. I have every faith in Ed's judgement,*" said Graham.

"*Do you want me to do anything, Ed?*" asked Captain Zoranski. "*No thanks,*" said Ed, "*we'll just let the team get on with it. We've rehearsed this several times and everyone knows exactly what they've got to do, so if you could kindly leave us to it, that'll be just fine.*" "*Very well. Shout of you need anything,*" said Zoranski.

Ed paused, "*On second thoughts, maybe you could just keep a watchful eye on the hangar doors, we don't want any hiccups there.*" Zoranski nodded. "*Not a problem, Ed. No-one else has the combination to get in here, I made sure of that.*"

Over in the unheated guard box at the entrance to the High Security Compound, the hatchet-faced and throroughly bored Duty Sergeant, Sergeant Grisha Vadick Chugunkin, was sat keeping himself occupied by blatantly blegging.

How he had ever reached the rank of Sergeant no-one could fathom. Totally lacking in ambition, he was dim, slovenly and over fed, and that was just for starters. Anything for a quiet life, that was Sergeant Chugunkin.

The Sergeant, the highest non-com in the compound, had been briefed earlier that day by Captain Zoranski that he'd been told by his superior, Major Orlov, that two trucks would be arriving at the compound later that evening, containing members of a 'snap' Security Inspection Team. They were to be given immediate access to the compound, no checks, no delays and no questions asked.

Other than that, Sergeant Chugunkin had been left in the dark. Like most other Russian commissioned officers, Captain Zoranski operated on the 'Need to Know' principle and as Sergeant Chugunkin didn't need to know anything else, he wasn't told anything else, so he just shrugged his shoulders and got on with it. In his little world, orders were orders.

The lack of information hadn't surprised Sergeant Chugunkin at all. Officers in the Russian military always played things very close to their chests and didn't deem it necessary to keep the lower ranks fully in the picture regarding anything. Soldiers were given just enough information to do their jobs, their superiors relying on the premise that knowledge was power.

After he'd been briefed, Sergeant Chugunkin had assembled the members of the guard nominated for compound and gate duty that evening and warned them about the impending security inspection. He'd cautioned them to be on their toes and also that they had to look as if they hadn't been pre-warned about the arrival of the 'snap' Security Inspection Team.

Chugunkin had thought that if the snap Security Inspection Team was supposed to be unexpected, then why would they be allowed straight into the compound without the usual checks? He was puzzled. It didn't make sense. Still, Captain Zoranski had told him what was required and that is precisely what would happen. His not to reason why.

Despite what his comrades thought of him, the Sergeant was not a complete simpleton and had sensed that something didn't ring quite true with the Captain's vague explanation. In addition, Sergeant Chugunkin had noticed that Captain Zoranski was sweating more than usual and looked decidedly shiftier than normal.

Although Captain Zoranski had been his usual semi-innebriated self, he hadn't seemed particularly concerned by the prospect of a snap security inspection, which Chugunkin thought a little strange. He knew that Zoranski usually went into the panic mode when he'd received a 'phone call from Major Orlov, which admittedly was a rare occurrence these days.

Peering out of the cracked guardroom window, Sergeant Chugunkin had witnessed the arrival of Ed's two trucks shortly after dusk, and noted that each vehicle had two people in their cabs, a driver and an escort.

"So, what sort of snap Security Inspection Team is this?" Chugunkin had asked himself, "one with only four people to inspect a place this size - and why are they not wearing uniform - and why have they arrived in two clapped out old trucks, not the usual UAZ-469's?" He came to the conclusion that, " That's a lot of why's. Something is not quite right here."

'The Russian UAZ-469'
'Off-road Light Utility Vehicle'

Suspicion gnawed at Chugunkin's brain to such an extent that after a while he decided to grasp the nettle and go above Captain Zorin's head. He would contact Zorin's superior officer, Major Orlov, for advice and guidance.

Chugunkin wasn't worried about doing that because he knew and had served with Major Orlov in Afghanistan way back when they were both much younger men and before their worlds had turned sour. Major Orlov had been Chugunkin's Platoon Lieutenant at the time.

Although never a particularly vibrant officer, the passed-over Major was now considered by virtually everyone as bordering on useless. Nevertheless, Chugunkin was certain that he could speak to the Major in confidence about his suspicions and that if he'd got it wrong then there wouldn't be any serious repercussions, other than perhaps receiving a verbal lashing. He could live with that. In one ear and out of the other.

Chugunkin picked up the telephone and rather grandly instructed the military operator to connect him to Major Orlov as a matter of extreme urgency, then sat there with the 'phone clamped to his ear, waiting impatiently for a response.

"Good evening, and to what do I owe this honour, Sergeant Chugunkin?" asked an obviously bored Orlov. *"Comrade Major, my apologies for disturbing you. Thank you for taking my call,"* said Sergeant Chugunkin. *"Not a problem, Chugsy. Now, what can I do for you?"*

"Comrade Major, I believe that something unusually suspicious is taking place within the compound here and I thought that you ought to know about it," said Chugunkin. A suddenly attentive Major Orlov asked, *"What do you mean something 'unusually suspicious' Chugsy?"*

"Well sir, a small snap Security Inspection Team, consisting of four people wearing civilian clothing, arrived here at the compound not ten minutes ago in two clapped out URAL-4320 trucks. They were met by my boss, Captain Zoranski, who took them straight into Hangar 2," said Chugunkin.

"Really. Please remind me, Chugsy, what is stored in Hangar 2 that is so important?" asked the Major. *"That, sir, is where, amongst many other valuables, the pallets of American dollars are secured,"* replied the Sergeant.

That snippet of information rang alarm bells in Major Orlov's head. Pallets of dollars - that struck a distant chord. He sat up and paid immediate attention. *"Pallets of American dollars you say? Explain yourself!"* ordered Major Orlov.

An eager Chugunkin continued, *"If I might respectfully remind you, Comrade Major, there are over 200 wooden pallets stored in Hangar 2, each of them containing one billion American dollars."*

Orlov's jaw dropped. *"Ah, yes, of course, it had slipped my mind. I do have many other such responsibilities you know, Chugsy!"* said Major Orlov, thinking to himself, *"That compound is so full of valuables and duty-free items that I can't possibly be expected to remember all of them."*

"And where is Captain Zoranski at this precise moment?" Orlov asked. *"He is accompanying the man in charge of the Security Inspection Team, Comrade Major."* replied Chugunkin. *"His name?"* snapped Major Orlov. *"Captain Rostislav Anatoly Zoranski, sir."*

Major Orlov sighed, *"I know 'his' name, Chugsy, you tit! What is the name of the officer heading the Security Inspection Team?"* *"I was not made privy to that information, sir, and the Captain took them straight inside the hangar,"* said a now chastened Sergeant Chugunkin.

"*What exactly is Zoranski doing there with them?*" asked a puzzled Orlov.

"*He took them and their two vehicles inside Hangar 2. The trucks are parked up next to the pallets on which the dollars are stacked - and sir, the main reason why I decided to call you was that one of the compound guards reported to me that he'd overheard a member of the Security Inspection Team chatting with Captain Zoranski in what he thought sounded like English!*" replied Chugunkin. "*My God, now that's interesting,*" said Major Orlov, his hands now trembling.

"*Huh, I didn't know that Zoranski could speak English. He can hardly string a sentence together in Russian on a normal day!*" thought Major Orlov.

"*What precisley are they doing in the Hangar?*" he asked Chugunkin. "*Don't know, sir. The doors of the hangar have now been closed so we are unable to see what's going on in there,*" said the Sergeant. "*Me and all of the lads were told to keep well out of the way by the Captain.*"

Orlov stood up, "*OK, Chugsy. Well done for getting in touch with me! I will look into this immediately. I should tell you that I know nothing of such an inspection.*"

Orlov continued, "*Now, listen very carefully, you are to secure the camp perimeter immediately. Turn out the full guard, but do it quietly, and make sure that they are all armed and carrying live ammunition - weapons to be locked and loaded. No-one, I repeat no-one is to be let either in or out of that compound without my express permission. Is that clear?"*

"*Yes, Comrade Major, crystal clear. I will give the order straight away!*" said a suddenly enthusiastic Chugunkin.

"*Good man, and Sergeant Chugunkin, you did absolutely the right thing by letting me know about this. There could be a promotion in this for you. Now, go and do your duty,*" instructed Orlov, before breaking the connection.

Orlov then sat and gathered his thoughts. "*Something is not quite right here. I'd better kick it upstairs!"*

Picking up the red telephone on his desk, Major Orlov snapped, "*Operator, this is Major Orlov. Connect me to Colonel Gregorovitch of the FSB, immediately. This is a 'Flash' priority call!*"

Within a few moments Colonel Gregorovitch had picked up his own telephone and answered. "*Good evening Major, er?" "Major Orlov speaking, Colonel."*

"*Ah yes, Orlov. What can I do for you, Major?*" asked Colonel Ivanski Gregorovitch, switching on the loudspeaker of his own 'phone so that his boss General Chelpinsky, who was sat at the side of him in an old leather armchair struggling to complete crossword in his copy of the Russian daily broadsheet 'Isvestia,' could hear what was being said.

"Comrade Colonel," said Orlov, *"I am seeking your advice. I have received an unusual report from the Duty Sergeant at the High Security Compound, Sheremetyevo Airport and I would like your guidance as to how you think I should proceed."*

"An unusual report you say?" asked the suddenly alert Colonel, *"Explain yourself!"*

"Yes, Comrade Colonel. The Sergeant informed me that a snap Security Inspection Team had turned up at the Compound out of the blue and was carrying out an inspection there. As you are no doubt aware, the two hangars in the compound are filled to the brim with money and valuables. Amongst other things it contains many billions of American dollars that have been palletised and stashed there under Presidential seal. I had heard on the grapevine that the money is the property of President Saddam Hussein." *"Yes, I am aware of that, Major,"* snapped Gregorovitch, although he wasn't.

General Chelpinski dropped his newspaper onto the floor of the office and beckoned for Gregorovitch to hand the 'phone over to him. *"This is General Chelpinski. Who am I speaking to?"* he asked.

"Jesus H Christ, it's 'Chiller' Chelpinski!" thought Major Orlov, his throat suddenly going very dry. He jumped to his feet then repeated, word for word, what he'd just told

Gregorovitch. "*Switch to standby for a moment, Major,*" Chelpinski ordered silkily, then placed his hand over the mouthpiece of the telephone.

Turning to Gregorovitch he asked, "*Ivanski, do you know if we have one of our Security Inspection Teams out tonight?*" "*Not as far as I'm aware, General. I can check it out with the Central Operations Room if you so wish,*" replied Gregorovitch. Chelpinski nodded, "*Yes, do that!*"

"*Incidentally, how far away from Headquarters is the compound?*" asked Chelpinski. "*It is situated just inside the Shermeteyov airport perimeter, about fifteen to twenty minutes by road from here, General*," replied Gregorovitch.

"*I'm having a senior moment, Ivanski, what precisely does the Security Compound contain?*" asked Chelpinski.

"*Well General, amongst other things it contains many billions of American dollars that have been palletised and stashed there under Presidential seal. I had heard on the grapevine that the money is the property of President Saddam Hussein.*" Chelpinsky nodded, "*Yes, now that you come to mention it, I'd heard that too.*"

Taking his hand off the telephone mouthpiece, Chelpinski said, "*Major Orlov, I have decided that in view of the potentiual seriousness of this incident, Colonel Gregorovitch and myself will come and investigate this matter personally. We will arrive outside the Security Compound in approximately twenty to thirty minutes.*

Where are you now?" he asked Orlov. *"I'm in my office, some fifteen minutes away from the compound, General,"* answered a now highly nervous Orlov.

"Well, you'd better get yourself across to the compound immediately - and make sure that you are armed. Do not under any circumstances allow anyone, and I mean anyone, in or out of that compound until myself and the Colonel arrive - is that clear?" *"Yes Comrade General, perfectly clear. I will make my way over to the compound immediately."* said Orlov.

Major Orlov realised that as a result of his 'phone call this thing was going big. He dreaded to think what 'Chiller' Chelpinski would do to him if it all turned out to be a storm in a tea-cup. His balls would be nailed to a Lubyanka Prison table.

"You are to wait for us at the main gate of the Security Compound and then I will personally re-assess the situation. Whatever happens, we will enter the compound mob-handed and sort this business out," instructed Chelpinski, before ringing off abruptly.

"At last, a bit of action, Ivanski," said a delighted Chelpinski, *"get on to the Duty Officer in the Central Operations Room. Have him check if one of our Security Inspection Team's has been scheduled to carry out a snap inspection of the compound this evening. If such a team has been tasked then there's nothing for us to worry about. If it doesn't, then there's something afoot."*

"And if there is no such team on the schedule, General?" asked Gregorovitch.

"Then instruct the Duty Officer that I require a Quick Reaction Platoon, fully tooled up and waiting outside the main entrance to this building within ten minutes, or heads will roll - including his!"

"I'll get straight onto it, General," replied Gregorovitch, striding off purposefully.

Back at the Security Compound, inside the hangar, the cross-loading of the pallets was very nearly completed, having gone much quicker than Ed had expected. The female lorry driver, Kostya Liochka, had proven to be a dab hand at operating the fork-lift and was just finishing loading the second truck.

The dummy pallets that they'd brought with them to Moscow had replaced the ones that had been sat on the floor of the hangar and the pallets containing the dollars had then been neatly stashed on-board Ed's two trucks. To all intents and purposes, the dummy pallets looked exactly like the ones that had held the dollars, which was the intention.

Once the side-curtains on the trucks had been secured and roped, no-one would be able to see what they contained. Similarly, no-one would have noticed the difference in the contents of the pallets on the hangar floor, not without inspecting them closely. That aspect had been well thought out and could prove to be a valuable delaying tactic.

Whilst Kostya had been unloading and then re-loading the trucks, her partner Artyon had helped the others to top up the voluminous fuel tanks of the URAL-4320's in readiness for the long flog from Moscow back to Saint Petersburg.

"*This is going much better than I expected, Ed,*" said Mike. "*Oy mouth - don't speak too soon,*" said Graham, "*you're the kiss of death!*" They both laughed.

At that precise moment the 'phone attached to the side of the hangar wall buzzed. Everyone froze. "*You'd better go and answer that,*" Ed said to Zoranski, "*see what they want. Play for time!*" Zoranski nodded and hurried over to answer it.

Zoranski picked up the 'phone, "*Captain Zoranski! What is it?*" As he listened to the voice replying from the other end of the 'phone, he mumbled something in reply then turned drip white.

"*There you are, I told you. Look at Zoranski's fizzog,*" said Graham, "*he looks as if he's lost a tenner and found a kopek! Call me old fashioned but if you ask me, the shit's just about to hit the fan!*"

Ed called out to Zoranski, "*What is it, my friend?*" "*My Sergeant has just informed me that an armed military convoy has arrived at the main gate and are demanding to come inside the compound,"* Zoranski replied.

"Were you expecting anyone tonight?" asked Ed. Zoranski shook his head, *"No, it is highly unusual." "Buggeration, I think we might have been rumbled!"* said Mike. *"Mike's right, they're onto us, Ed!"* said Graham.

"So, let's stay cool and revert to 'Plan B' then," said Ed. *"What is your 'Plan B'?* called out a flustered Zoranski. *"Simple,"* said Ed, *"our trucks and the guys just hot-foot it out of the compound."* *"And what about us four?"* asked Zoranski, *"We'll jump on board the 'T3-Travellator' and do the same,"* said Ed.

"And what about those guys at the gate, won't they try and stop the trucks?" asked Mike. *"That's a chance we'll have to take,"* said Ed. He called out to Zoranski, *"Do you know how many men are at the gate?"* Zoranski spoke to his caller then replaced the 'phone back on its stand. *"He said that there's about about thirty of them."*

"Why the hell has a military convoy suddenly arrived at the compound gates - and more importantly, what do they want?" Graham asked. *"Perhaps they're here to do what we were pretending to do - carry out a security check?"* said Mike hopefully.

"I hardly think so, they are armed and have two very senior officers accompanying them," said Captain Zoranski, just as the 'phone on the wall buzzed again.

He lifted the 'phone from its cradle and heard a familiar voice, "*Captain Zoranski*," the voice said. "*this is Major Orlov speaking. I am handing the 'phone over to General Chelpinsky who wishes to speak with you!*"

On hearing the name 'General Chelpinski,' Zoranski felt his legs weaken and he would have fallen to the floor if Ed hadn't supported him. "*What is it?*" asked Ed. Zoranski whispered, "*General 'Chiller' Chelpinsky is here - we are doomed!*"

Ed placed his ear next to the 'phone so that he could listen closely to what was being said. His nose wrinkeld as he smelled the sweat of fear oozing out of Zoranski's pores.

"*Captain Zoranski, are you there?*" A nervous Zoranski replied, "*Yes, I am here.*" Chelpinsky continued, "*This is General Chelpinsky. I am speaking to you from the telephone at the main gate. You are to exit the hangar and make your way over to the guardroom immediately. I wish to speak with you face to face and I would advise you not to keep me waiting!*"

"*I am on my way, General,*" said Zoranski, then rang off. He turned to Ed and said, "*Like hell I am!*" "*It's that bloody man General Chelpinski,*" said Ed, grimacing "*Turns up like the proverbial bad penny,*" said Mike, "*And I'll bet you a pound to a pinch of shite that he's got 'Ivan the Terrible' in tow!*"

Zoranski turned to Ed, "*Now we are in big trouble. You know who that is…*" Ed interrupted, "*Yes, General Chel-*

bloody-pinski. Unfortunately we've met him before, a very long time ago when he was a mere Lieutenant Colonel."

"Then you know that the game is well and truly up. We might as well surrender now. Chelpinski is a ruthless, star spangled bastard!" said Zoranski.

"No way are we surrendering, especially to that murderous swine," said Ed. *"So what steps do we take now?"* asked Mike. *"Fookin' big ones!"* said Graham.

"Stay calm, my friends," said Ed, *"this is what we're going to do. Captain Zoranski, call your guards and order them to keep the main gate closed and not to let anyone in. Tell them that those people dressed as soldiers and claiming to be military are trying to get into the compound in order to rob it. They are not to allow them in here under any circumstances!"*

"And then what?" asked Zoranski.

"We can't risk breaking out of the front gate with that lot waiting for us, so we'll use whatever time we have left to break through the back of the hangar wall, punch a hole through the perimeter fencing at the rear of the compound and then the two trucks can head for the highway."

"It's a bit of a dog's dinner, but that's 'Plan B'" said Ed, *"and as soon as our trucks have broken out of here, me, you, Ed and Graham will jump on board the 'T-3' and head for home."*

As they were speaking, the doors of the Hangar started to rumble slowly open. *"What the hell?"* said Zoranski. As the doors partially opened, they revealed a mean looking Sergeant Chugunkin, who was pointing his rifle directly at them. It was obvious that he meant business.

Zoranski suddenly remembered that the Duty Sergeant also held the combinations for all of the compound's security systems. He could have kicked himself for forgetting that key bit of information.

"Gentlemen," Chugunkin shouted, *"I would advise you to come out of there with your hands in the air. Come on! The game is up! Move yourselves or I will open fire!"* he shouted.

"I might have guessed it!" hissed Zoranski, *"That greasy, boot-licking swine Chugunkin is obviously at the back of all this!"* Zoranski shouted, *"Lower your weapon, Sergeant. There is not a problem. I am coming out to speak to you! This has all been part of a security test! Lower your weapon, now!"*

An unsuspecting and puzzled looking Chugunkin slowly lowered his weapon.

Zoranski surreptitiously slid his pistol out of its holster, then suddenly turning sideways on he raised his arm and aimed the pistol at Chugunkin then shot him twice in the chest. Zoranski was more surprised than Chugunkin that his weapon had fired - he hadn't cleaned it for months.

The shocked and now mortally wounded Chugunkin was knocked backwards by the force of the bullets hitting him and fell backwards onto the hangar floor, but still managed to loose off a spray of bullets towards the corner of the Hangar, completely missing Zoranski and the rest, but hitting the 'T3-Travellator,' badly damaging it.

Several chunks of metal were ripped off the now shredded outer casing of the 'T3', other rounds zipping around the hangar like angry wasps. The door of the 'T3' was hanging off its hinges at a crazy angle. The all-important 'Time-Machine' was plainly very badly damaged.

Zoranski fired again, this time hitting the Sergeant in the forehead, killing him instantly. He then ran across to the hangar entrance, rolled the Sergeant outside then reached across and tapped in the code on the electronic security key pad and the hangar doors started to close.

"*We don't have very long, Comrades, I can see others running towards us,*" he shouted. The hangar doors slid shut.

Graham, looked across at the smoking 'T3-Travellator' now peppered with bullet holes, and said, "*That's bollocksed it right up - look at the state of the 'T3' it's like a string vest. We can't risk travelling in it now!*"

"*So what's the alternative then?*" Mike asked. "*We stay calm and use what's left of the fuel in those jerricans to set light to the 'T3' and then we'll jump on board the trucks and leave with them,*" said Ed.

"*Burn the 'T3?'*" said Mike. Ed nodded, "*Yes, burn it. We don't want the Russians getting their sticky hands on an operational 'T-3.' It has to be made totally unusable!*"

"*OK, I'll see to that myself,*" volunteered Mike, running across to the 'T3,' pausing to collect a full jerrycan of fuel along the way.

He flipped the jerrycan's cap open then proceeded to splash fuel all over the outside of the battered 'T3-Travellator' before throwing the half empty can inside it, the fuel spilling out across the floor.

Mike pulled a handkerchief out of his pocket, dipped it in the fuel, lit it then threw it inside the 'T3' and stepped back quickly. There was a loud 'whoosh' as the fuel ignited. Within a few seconds the 'T3' was burning fiercely and the innards were being consumed rapidly by the belching flames. "*Och, what a shocking waste!*" said Mike, shaking his head.

Above the noise of the burning 'T-3' Ed's trained ear heard the crackle of gunfire coming from outside the hangar and rounds clanging off the outside of the metal door. They were under attack and Ed knew that they didn't have much time left. General Chelpinski had obviously lost patience and ordered his men into the compound then across to the hangar.

Ed turned to Chelpinski and said, "*Before we start demolishing the place, I'm right in assuming that there's not a back way out of the hangar?*" An alarmed looking

Zoranski shook his head, *"No, of course not, this is a secure building. Only one way in and the same way out!"*

"OK," said Ed, *"then, like I said, we'll just have to punch a hole in the back wall with the fork-lift and escape that way." "And after that, then what happens?"* asked an increasingly desperate Zoranski.

"We'll ram our way through the outer perimeter fence, get onto the highway, then head out of Moscow as fast as we can. With a bit of luck and a fair wind we'll be well on our way by the time opposition gets past the front door of the hangar and realises what's happened." said Ed.

"They might hear us smashing a hole in the wall though! What if they're outside waiting for us?" asked Graham.

Captain Zoranski shook his head, *"That would be difficult my friend. They'll have to get in via the front entrance to the hangar, they won't be able to get down the sides of it,"* he said, *"It's all been sealed off with razor wire and it is mined. As far as they are concerned, the only way in and out of here is through those front doors!"*

Sprinting faster than he had for years, Captain Zoranski thrashed across to the flashing electronic key pad mounted on the wall by the hangar doors and smashed it to pieces with the butt of his pistol. *"That might help to delay things,"* he shouted.

Strangely enough, for the first time in many years Zoranski was starting to enjoy himself. His adrenaline was racing and suddenly he felt good.

A few minutes earlier, all hell had broken loose at the front gate leading into the compound when General Chelpinski had pulled rank and demanded that the gates be opened. The confused and suspicious gate guards, who knew absolutely nothing about what was going on, had refused to let either him or his men inside without authority from Captain Zoranski.

Major Orlov screamed at them until he was red in the face, but they still refused to obey him.

The General had warned the gate guards that the soldiers accompanying him would be ordered to open fire if the gate was not opened and the barrier raised immediately. The twitchy gate guards still refused to open the gates and replied that they would open fire on the General and his men if they made any threatening moves.

The confused gate guards mistakenly thought that this could well be part of some sort of security test and didn't want to be the ones to be found wanting. They couldn't ask their Sergeant for guidance because he'd legged it over to Hangar 2 to find out what was going on in there. So, when in doubt - they obeyed the last order, which had come from Captain Zoranski! Stand fast!

'*Always obey the last order!*' was what the Russian soldiers had been trained to do, and as their Officer had ordered them not to let anyone in or out of the compound, that's precisely what they did. "*Anyway,*" one of them said, "*anyone could claim to be a bloody General!*" They'd all been warned not to fall for that sort of wheeze. The old adage sprang to mind, "*Order, then Counter-order, leads to Disorder.*"

Just as they'd decided not to do anything, they heard the sound of shooting coming from the hangar area, adding to the general confusion.

Drawing his pistol, General Chelpinski shouted, "*Ivanski, order the Captain of the QRP (Quick Reaction Platoon) to get that damned compound gate rammed open - now!*" Gregorovitch ran across to the QRP Captain and passed on the General's order.

The truck that had accompanied Chelpinski and Gregorovitch disgorged its infanteers, then the driver revved the engine up, slammed it into gear and hurtled towards the main gate, closely followed on foot by the QRP, using the vehicle as cover.

As the compound gates were smashed aside, General Chelpinski cocked his pistol, ran up to the guard post and without any further warning, shot two of the gate guards dead. "*Bloody idiots!*" he snarled.

All hell broke loose, with the remaining compound guards opening fire on the QRP and the QRP returning far more effective and accurate fire on the compound guards.

The compound guards soon realised that they were no match for the deadly efficient QRP, who had spread out and were ducking and diving in every direction, firing at the compound guards indiscriminately. Realising that they were badly outnumbered and dropping like flies, the compound guards laid down their weapons and raised their hands in abject surrender.

"I am General Chelpinsky! Pick up your weapons you idiots and follow the QRP over to the hangar!" roared Chelpinsky. *"To the Hangar, men!"* shouted Colonel Gregorovitch, *"Quickly, there is not a moment to lose!"*

The now thoroughly confused compound guards retrieved their weapons and ran after the QRP soldiers.

Back inside Hangar 2, Kostya Liochka had smashed a huge hole in the Hangar's rear wall, using the fork-lift truck as a battering ram. She'd revelled in the naked aggression of it all and had laughed loudly as she'd smashed the fabric of the wall to shreds. The fork-lift was now a smoking ruin.

Once the hole had been made large enough for the two cargo trucks to drive through easily, she'd begrudgingly parked the severely dented fork-lift up in the corner of the hangar and returned to her own truck, giving Ed the thumbs up.

"OK, line 'em up then! Time to get out of here" shouted Ed.

"Bloody hell, did you see what she did to that wall, Graham?" said Mike, *"I wouldnae like tae to meet yon Kostya when she was indulging in a wee spot of road rage, you ken what I mean!"* Graham nodded, *"Just my sort of chick - tattooed, rough and ready!"* he said.

"Right, on board the trucks everyone, quick as you can!" shouted Ed, *"Captain, you come with me in the first truck, Graham, you and Mike get on board the second truck with Artyom. Remind Artyom to leave his truck lights off until we get a couple of clicks down the highway,"* he said, *"and I'll remind Kostya to do the same."*

Turning to his two sons, Ed said, *"Deiderick, Ludo, you two jump in the back of one of the trucks. Come on, let's get out of here!"*

As he headed towards his truck, Mike looked back wistfully across at the 'T3-Travellator' which was burning merrily away and filling the hangar with thick, black smoke. He said, *"Bloody hell, there's a good thirty million quid gone down straight doon the khazi! How am I going to explain that one to Liverpool Victoria!"*

The engines of the two URAL-4320 Cargo Trucks that had been idling, roared into life, then truck number one, closely followed by truck number two, their passengers safely on board and loads secured, moved slowly towards the newly opened hangar exit, their engines now grunting powerfully. Ed turned to Kostya and said, *"OK, hit the gas Kostya, and let's get rolling!"*

Both of the very experienced drivers gently eased their trucks out of the secure hangar, edging over the rubble and trundling their way across the grass towards the outer perimeter fence, driving carefully in the dark. Fortunately the perimeter lights didn't cover that area.

Captain Zoranski pointed through the gloom at a section of the wire fence that ran alongside the highroad and ordered Kostya to, *"Hurry, we do not have much time; the rear wall of the secure hangar will conceal our escape for only a short while longer. Break through at that point over there!"*

Ed nodded, *"Go for it, Kostya!"* Kostya, grinned wolfishly and hit the accelerator, then slammed her truck into the perimeter fence, swatting it out of the way as if it was made of rice paper. This whole thing was turning out to be much more fun than she'd expected - she was a warrior at heart and loved a bit of action.

The second truck, driven by Kostya's beloved, followed closely on her tail, then both trucks bounced onto the smooth tarmac and roared off up the road at a great rate of knots, everyone hanging on for grim death.

Mike turned to Graham and said, *"Bloody good job that there's nae trenches or monsoon drains for us to vault across!"* *"This is Moscow, not Malaysia!"* replied Graham.

After they'd travelled a couple of kilometres along the highway the two drivers switched their vehicle's headlights on and motored on, blending in with the other sparse traffic. Ed kept looking in the truck's rear-view mirror to see if they were being followed by the Russian's which much to his relief they didn't appear to be, not yet anyway.

Ed knew that it would only be a matter of time before the Russians caught up with them and that's when then the real fun and games would start. Ed wished that they'd brought some weapons with them. A couple of grenades would have come in exceedingly handy. All they had was the Captain's pistol, and that was now three rounds down.

They'd considered bringing weapons at the initial planning stages of the operation, but thought that as they'd be in and out of the compound safely, under the umbrella of protection provided by Captain Zoranski, that they wouldn't need guns. Bad decision.

Mike and Graham had made themselves as comfortable as they could in the large cab of the second truck and seemed to be getting on swimmingly with the driver, the muscle-bound Artyom Bogdanovitch. Had he not been a part of the team, though, then the lads would definitely have found his presence rather intimidating.

In truth, Artyom was something of a gentle giant, but with his shaven head, work-house shovel hands, shoulders covered in colourful tattoos and with at least three of his front teeth missing, he looked scary and definitely not someone to be tampered with.

Artyom's English was very basic, so when Graham whispered to Mike, *"That lass of his looks a bit on the wild side, and did you see that blemish on her chin, Mike."* Artyom just smiled disarmingly at them and concentrated on his driving, seeming to not understand them.

Mike replied, *"The blemish? Nae problem. As they say in Glasgow, Graham, when a man is in love, a wart seems like a dimple."* Artyom's face was the very essence of concentration as he closely followed the lead truck, driven by his beloved, Kostya.

After a few moments, Artyom turned to Graham and, after elbowing him in the ribs, said, *"Hey English, Mike is quite right - if you really love your chick, then a wart does seem like a dimple. Yes, I like that!"* then he roared with laughter.

Graham blushed and the journey continued in silence.

Ж

CHAPTER SIX

'TALLY-HO!'

The Russian QRP had well and truly thinned out the security compound guards, whose ranks had been decimated in the short, sharp conflict; the few guards that had survived the encounter had soon realised that they were up against highly trained professionals, so had thrown down their weapons and raised their hands, surprisingly only to be ordered to pick them up again by a puce-faced bellowing senior officer, and then told to join forces with the QRP.

A manic General Chelpinski had sprinted across to Hangar 2, noting that it was still secure. As he didn't have access to the security code to get the hangar door open, and eager to get inside, he instructed Colonel Gregorovitch to order the driver of the QRP truck to ram the hangar doors wide open with his vehicle.

The QRP truck reversed back several feet, the driver revved the engine then the vehicle hurtled forward, slamming into the hangar doors, smashing them open. Unfortunately, Sergeant Chugunkin, who was laid on the floor directly in the path of the oncoming truck, was shredded by the truck's huge wheels, but as he was quite dead, fortunately didn't feel a thing.

Once inside the Hangar, the first thing Chelpinski spotted was the smoking ruins of the 'T3-Travellator'' the shape of which, for some reason he couldn't fathom, looked vaguely familiar to him. He also clocked the very large hole that had been punched into the rear hangar wall and ran across to examine it. The hole gaped back at him like the mouth of a corpse.

Chelpinski realised immediately that it had been used as an emergency exit. The grass outside had been mashed up by the tyres of the two trucks, the deep gouges on the grass leading straight towards the perimeter fence, which he noted had also been smashed aside.

Colonel Gregorovitch, who was examining the 'dummy' pallets, shouted, *"General, these pallets over here are empty!"*

"The thieving swine must have transferred the money to their vehicles. Quickly, Ivanski, we must chase after them. They have to be stopped!" replied Chelpinski.

"We can't use the QRP truck, General," said Ivanski. *"Why not?"* roared Chelpinsky. *"Because the radiator was damaged beyond repair when the truck smashed its way through the hangar doors."* said Ivanski.

"Well, we'll follow them in my UAZ-469 then! Go and get it!" hollered Chelpinsky, *"and grab a couple of the QRP boys then we'll get after those thieving bastards; they can't be that far away. Oh, and tell the useless Major Orlov to get onto Central Headquarters and update them on what's happened here. He is to tell them that we need reinforcements here - now!"*

"We will leave Major Orlov and the QRP officer here to secure this place and get some road-blocks organised! Tell him!" commanded Chelpinski.

Gregorovitch nodded, calling Major Orlov and the Officer Commanding the QRP across for their new orders, whilst General Chelpinski sloped across the hangar to examine the smoking ruins of the 'T3-Travellator.'

As he was nosing around, he called out to Gregorovitch, *"Ivanski, over here, please!"* Gregorovitch ran over to Chelpinski, *"General?"* Chelpinski pointed at the remnants of the 'T3' and said quietly:

"Ivanski, cast your mind back a few years to the early 1960's, the cellars of the Lubyanka Prison to be precise, when you and I were trapped inside the 'Hidden Library." He pointed at the 'T-3,' *"Does that heap of smouldering crap remind you of anything?"* asked the General.

Ivanski looked at the smouldering heap of metal, wood and plastic that had been the 'T3' for a moment or two and as the scales fell from his eyes he nodded and replied,

"Yes, now that you mention it, it does look vaguely familiar, General, but I can't quite put my finger on why."

Ivanski examined the smoking wreckage more closely then said, *"Of course - got it! It's a 'T-3 Travellator, is it not, General?"* Chelpinski nodded, *"Correct! Well done, Ivanski. And the next question you should be asking yourself is why is it here in this hangar?"*

Colonel Gregorovitch looked puzzled. *"Sorry General, I'm afraid you've lost me."*

Chelpinski continued, *"I have a nagging suspicion, Ivanski, that those 'Time-Travelling' bastards have staged a re-appearance and have been here up to their usual thieving mischief - but this time they won't get away with it!"* *"Of course,"* said Ivanski, *"Why didn't I think of that!"* General Chelpinski replied sarcastically, *"You will, eventually! Now, the vehicle, Ivanski, quickly!"*

The UAZ-469 skidded to a halt outside the hangar, its wheels squealing dramatically on the tarmac. *"Come on then, let's get moving!"* roared General Chelpinski as he ran towards the vehicle.

Chelpinski threw himself into the front passenger seat of the UAZ-469, at the same time ordering the driver out of the vehicle, *"Get out! Colonel Gregorovitch will drive!"* Ivanski pushed the driver out of the way, jumped into to the driving seat and revved the engine. He was loving every second of the drama.

"*Let's go, Ivanski!*" ordered the General. "*Where to, sir?*" Ivanski asked. "*Oh, let me think now. They tell me that the centre of Moscow is rather lovely at this time of year,*" said Chelpinsky.

Chelpinsky pointed at the gaping hole in the back of the hangar and roared, "*Through there - then follow the vehicle tracks that lead to the road! Catch up with the trucks that made those tracks and there's a medal in this for you!*"

Ivanski slammed the UAZ-469 into gear and, clinging on for grim death, they roared off out of the rear of the hangar, bouncing across the grass towards the hole in the perimeter fence. As he was wrestling with the steering wheel, Ivanski noticed that there was a strong smell of fuel, but in the heat of the moment chose to ignore it.

"*Come on Ivanski, get your bloody boot down. They can't be that far ahead!*" ordered Chelpinski.

Ж

CHAPTER SEVEN

'THE COMRADE SUPREME COMMANDER REQUIRES YOUR PRESENCE!'

Deep inside the Senate Building of the huge Moscow Kremlin complex, was Russian President Baronovski's lush office, where all was far from well. If a pin had dropped, the sound of it hitting the floor would have sounded like a metal dustbin lid hitting the pavement.

Boris Baronovski, President of Russia and Supreme Commander of the Armed Forces, was in yet another of his infamous and regular foul moods. The problem was that his ego and reputation had been dented.

Word had recently reached his 'Doctor Spock' like ears that somehow the High Security Compound at Moscow's Sheremetyevo Airport had been breached by person or persons unknown and 26 pallets of American dollars, worth something in the region of $26 billion in total, had been stolen.

The money had been held there in storage there for a number of years on behalf of the President's dear and closest friend, ex-President Saddam Hussein.

Baronovski was spitting feathers. The theft of the money had caused the Russian President a huge loss of face and as a consequence he had thrown his teddy in the corner and was now thirsting for revenge.

Ex-President Saddam Hussein himself had never trusted banks, having seen for himself just how easy it was to rob them, but after having been assured by his best friend, the Russian President, that the High Security Compound at Sheremetyevo Airport was as impenetrable as America's Fort Knox, had decided to take the President at his word and store the majority of his ill-gotten gains there.

"He placed his trust in us and this is how we repay that trust! Make no mistake, I will have someone's guts for garters for this!" Baronovski had roared. He could be heard shouting all over the Kremlin.

Initially, when he'd been been informed of the robbery, President Baronovski had turned white with anger, lost all control and showed the unfortunate Colonel who had delivered the bad news to him the hairy side of his hand, knocking him spinning across the presidential office.

Unfortunately the bearer of bad news always got it in the neck (or in the Colonel's case - the face)! The unfortunate Colonel had been dismissed from the President's office with his lips and nose bleeding and the threat of being posted to North Korea ringing in his ears.

On receiving the news, Baronovski had immediately summoned his recently appointed Leader of Soviet

Security and Intelligence Services, General Ivanski 'Chiller' Chelpinski, to his Kremlin office to explain what had happened and to ask him how he intended resolving the unsatisfactory and embarrassing situation. The President wanted to know just what Chelpinski was going to do to retrieve the stolen money and also arrest the impertinent thieves who had had the temerity to steal it in the first place.

Directly above the large, highly decorated and ornate gilded double doors leading into the President's office, just beneath the impressive central wall-mounted solid gold Imperial Russian Eagle, was an innocuous looking box-shaped electronic '*Wait - Enter'* sign, activated by a button on the President's desk.

Visitors standing outside the door waiting to meet the President were under constant covert surveillance by a discreetly hidden CCTV camera, placed inside the box containing the sign. The President also had a TV monitor built into his desk so that he could watch who was there waiting to see him.

Irrespective of their importance in the scheme of things, the President took a perverse delight in keeping visitors waiting. He knew that it added to their unease and unsettled them, which he thought gave him the whip hand.

He had, famously, once kept the American President stood waiting outside his officer for ten minutes, but that had backfired badly as the fiesty American had taken offence and swept out of the Kremlin in high dudgeon. It had taken a lot of sweet talking and the offer of trade deals by a flapping Baronovski to get the American to return.

The recently promoted and rather self-important General Chelpinski was lurking outside the President's office, filled with apprehension, waiting for the electronic sign to change, signifying that he could enter.

Chelpinsky realised that the next few minutes weren't going to be particularly pleasant for him and that his feet were about to be held to the fire because of the robbery and his failure to capture the thieves.

The sign above the door was currently indicating – '**Wāt**' (*Wait*). When the '**Wāt**' light was displayed, no-one dared enter the President's office, unless it was a matter of life or death. Chelpinski's eyes were glued to the sign because once the light signified that access was permitted, only then was it safe to enter.

You had to get your arse in gear once the light changed, as it did not do to keep the notoriously impatient President Baronovski waiting, particularly if he was in a foul mood, like he was today. Chelpinski could hear his own stomach gurgling and hoped that it wasn't too noticeable.

Suddenly, the sign blinked from red to white, changing to read – '**Voyti**' (*Enter*). As if by magic, the two immaculately uniformed Kremlin Regiment armed sentries stood guarding the doors, turned smartly inwards and in complete unison heaved the heavy doors silently open.

'Members of the Kremlin Regiment'

Chelpinski, who had been in the President's office only a few months previously under completely different circumstances, (when he'd been handed his General's shoulder rank slides personally by the President and had shared more than a glass or two of celebratory vodka with him), was not looking forward to the next few minutes.

This meeting, Chelpinski knew, was definitely classed as being one 'without vodka.' The General took a deep breath then strode through the doors leading into the lion's den.

The doors closed silently behind him as he marched across the office and halted smartly in front of the President's desk, praying that his boots wouldn't slip on the deeply waxed parquet flooring, then saluted.

There was a deathly silence as the President, who was gazing down at his blotting pad, completely ignored him.

The tight-lipped President, the complete Alpha male, then leaned back in his chair and stared at General Chelpinski for a further full minute, his icy light-blue eyes missing nothing. His fists were clenched before him on the desk and he was clearly fighting to gain control of his notoriously bad temper.

Chelpinsky knew full well that if the President's fists were clenched, it was a bad sign and that it was best just to keep one's mouth firmly closed and try to weather the storm.

Baronovski's fist were clenched so tightly that his knuckles were white. Chelpinski waited with trepidation for the inevitable explosion.

Rather surprisingly, the President suddenly unclenched his fists, breathed out slowly and then said, quite calmly, *"Take a seat, General!"* A surprised Chelpinski sat to attention in the high-backed chair that was placed immediately in front of the President's voluminous and highly polished desk.

Still nothing was said by the President for a few moments. *"Where is all this going?"* thought an uncomfortable Chelpinsky.

After a further nerve-twanging minute, the President spoke, *"You are no doubt aware, General Chelpinski, that I abhor time wasting, so I will get straight to the point."*

"I have been informed that the so-called High Security Compound at Sheremetyevo Airport has been breached for the first time in living memory and that a vast sum of money stored there on behalf of my dear and closest comrade, President Saddam Hussein, has been removed. Why has that been allowed to happen, I ask myself?!"

General Chelpinski started to respond but the President slammed his fist onto the desk, startling Chelpinski and silencing him, *"Do not have the impertinence to interrupt me when I am asking what is quite plainly a rhetorical question, General! I do not have the time, nor do I have the patience to listen to apologist waffle!"*

The President continued icily, *"I note that you personally and, I might add, somewhat negligently, managed to lose track of the compound thieves somewhere on the outskirts of Moscow on the highway leading to Saint Petersburg!"*

Chelpinski decided that it was safe to speak, *"They were within spitting distance and I very nearly apprehended them, Mister President, er Comrade Supreme Commander, but during the initial fire-fight to get into the Secure Compound...."* interrupting him, the President snorted and said dismissively, *"Secure Compound - huh, something of a misnomer I think!"*

Chelpinsky battled valiantly on, *"During the fire-fight at the High Security Compound at Sheremetyevo Airport, we didn't know it then but a stray bullet had punctured the fuel tank of our only serviceable vehicle, the one we used for the chase, which unfortunately ran out of fuel after some thirty kilometres, so we were unable to continue the pursuit,"* said a now thoroughly chastened and miserable General Chelpinsky, his head bowed.

"*Could you not have commandeered another vehicle, General? I'm sure that the Russian Army must have many other vehicles at it's disposal?*" queried the President.

Chelpinsky shook his head, "*I regret to say that we didn't have a radio with us, Comrade Supreme Commander, such was our hurry to get after the thieves. Reinforcements were on the way, but had not reached us at that stage.*"

He continued, "*Regrettably, the only other vehicle on the road at the time was an ancient clapped-out tractor hauling a trailer full of turnips, so it would have been a waste of time commandeering it.*"

"*Turnips! Turnips! I do not want to hear about turnips! This goes from bad to worse!*" grumbled Baronovski, "*Continue!*" he ordered.

Chelpinsky forged ahead, "*I sent one of my men to a nearby farmhouse and he eventually managed to summon a replacement vehicle, but by the time it arrived we had lost sight of the two trucks. I now believe that they managed to evade us by slipping off the main highway and onto one of the many side-roads.*"

Chelpinsky's mouth was very dry. He would have sold his soul, if he'd had one, for a sip of water.

"Well, it doesn't take the brains of an Archbishop to realise that this whole thing has been a star spangled cock-up from start to finish, wouldn't you agree, General?" said the President. A shame-faced looking General Chelpinski nodded in agreement.

President Baronovski sat back, gave Chelpinski a withering glance then, surprising Chelpinsky, sighed and said, *"Very well, I will give you the benefit of the doubt on this one occasion, General. I suppose that this sort of misfortune could happen to any one of us."*

He continued, *"Don't look so down in the mouth. As you well know, Comrade, being a General is not all about parades, pretty uniforms, jangling medals and saluting! My predecessor used to say, 'You eat the steak - you pay for it!' Although of course he doesn't get to eat steak where he is currently residing!"*

Chelpinsky nodded, thinking, *"Here it comes, the punch-line."*

The President then leaned forward, slammed his hand on the desk, startling Chelpinsky, and said pointedly, *"I want the perpetrators of this theft to be rounded up at the earliest opportunity and every single dollar of President Husseins's stolen money returned!"*

He continued, *"Everyone involved in this robbery, including those on the periphery, must be arrested, along with all of the so-called 'guards' at the compound and their supervising officers - who, incidentally, are to be replaced immediately."*

"That has already been done, Comrade Supreme Commander. The Officer-in-charge has been placed in close-arrest. His Second-in-command, whom we suspect is a leading member of the gang, will, I can assure you, be joining him very shortly!" said Chelpinski.

"Their names?" asked the President. *"The Officer-in-charge is a Major Leonid Vikto Orlov," "And his Second-in-command?"* said Baronovski. *"Captain Rostislav Anatoly Zoranski, Comrade Supreme Commander."*

The President continued, *"Those traitorous officers who were in charge of the guard detachment at the compound are to receive 'special' treatment once they have been thoroughly interrogated, as an example to others, if nothing else. Understand?"* Chelpinsky nodded again.

Chelpinsky plucked up the courage to speak again, trying his best to sound more confident than he felt, *"The Officer-in-charge, Major Orlov, Comrade Supreme Commander, is I believe at this stage guilty only of gross inefficiency. I am certain that he did not profit from the robbery."*

"Continue," ordered the President.

"It would appear that the brains and main perpetrator behind the robbery was Orlov's Second-in-Command, Captain Zoranski. Let me assure you, Comrade Supreme

Commander that the net is rapidly closing in on Zoranski," said Chelpinsky.
The President nodded, *"Good! Fortunately for us all, President Saddam, to whom the money belongs, is currently tucked away in my holiday dacha at Cape Idokopas on the Black Sea Coast, near the beautiful village of Praskoveeka in Gelendzhik, Krasnodar Krai and will not be returning to Moscow for three whole weeks. Hopefully he will not yet have heard anything of this farce."*

'President Baronovski's little Holiday Dacha'

Baronovski continued, *"General, I have decided that you will have just one week, starting from today, to resolve this situation to my complete satisfaction. If you fail to do so, you and your senior staff will suffer the dire consequences."*

Adopting his best 'whipped cur' look, Chelpnisky nodded as the President continued, *"This matter is to be brought to a swift and satisfactory conclusion. If you are unable to achieve that, then let me assure you that the very first thing to happen is that you will be removed from your post immediately and reduced in rank from General to private soldier - before you can say Vladimir Putin! Do I make myself clear?"* he shouted angrily, thumping the desk again with his bunched fist.

A humbled and red-faced General Chelpinsky, sweat trickling down his now stiffened spine, nodded and replied, *"Crystal clear, Comrade Supreme Commander!"*

The President nodded and continued, *"You have my authority to resolve this situation in any way that you see fit! Nothing and no-one is to be allowed to stand in your way! Here, show this letter of Presidential authority to anyone who has the stupidity to try to stand in your way!"*

The President slid a signed piece of crested notepaper across the desk towards Chelpinsky, who reached forward and scooped it up. He glanced at it quickly then folded it in half and placed it in his jacket pocket. *"I will guard this precious document with my life, Comrade Supreme Commander,"* he said.

The President nodded, *"One more thing, Chelpinski, remember that I am speaking to you today not as your President but as the Commander-in-Chief of the Russian Armed Forces. This situation is not some political snafu that can just be covered up and forgotten about, this is a military matter and my reputation is at stake."*

Baronovski turned and looked at the wall-clock as it started to chime, *"As you can hear, time moves on, so you'd better get your arse in gear. Understand?"*

"I understand fully, Comrade Supreme Commander," said General Chelpinski. The President waved his hand, *"Get out!"* Leaping to his feet, saluting then turning swiftly, Chelpinsky marched towards the door leading out of the office. *"I want results, General!"* snapped the President.

As Chelpinski marched towards the magnificent doors, they swung open as if by magic. It was all very simple really, the President had a button by his foot that when tapped sent a signal to the guards earpieces so that they knew when to open the doors.

Sometimes Baronovski amused himself by not tapping the button for a few moments and watching those waiting to leave lurking helplessly by the doors. It gave him a childish sense of superiority. Today though, he just wanted to see the back of General Chelpinsky.

Once outside the President's inner sanctum and out of sight of his searingly soul-searching gaze, the General paused to wipe a thin bead of sweat from his top lip, using his jacket sleeve.

Chelpinski noticed that, unusally for him, his hands and legs were trembling. *"One damned week! Who does he think I am, Rodion Meglin!"* muttered Chelpinski, before stomping off.

(*) – Rodion Meglin – a famous Russian Detective.

Once the General had marched off and disappeared out of sight, the two soldiers guarding the doors leading to the

President's office glanced across at each other and sniggered.

"Someone's had his feet well and truly sharpened!" said one. The other guard nodded in agreement, *"You may not have registered it, Comrade, but that 'someone' was the infamous General Chelpinsky!"* The other guard gasped, *"Not 'Chiller' Chelpinski of the FSB?"* His mate nodded, *"Yes, 'Chiller' Chelpinski. Huh, now there's a crime against humanity if ever there was one!"*

His mate nodded in agreement and whispered, *"Yes, there's a man who if you invited him to dinner you'd have to count the spoons afterwards. Better that he'd been strangled at birth!"*

Ж

CHAPTER EIGHT

'NEARLY THERE'

After making one very short stop near a small town called Krettsky in order to stretch their legs and check their vehicles over for the final leg of the journey, Ed's small convoy had reached the outskirts of Velicky Novgorod without any trouble.

After leaving the main highway at the earliest suitable opportunity, Ed's two URAL-4320 cargo trucks were now hidden away in a lay-by, out of sight behind some leafy trees. The all important truck drivers, Artyom and Kostya, were taking a short but much needed rest break whilst the others refuelled the trucks, chucking the empty jerricans behind the lay-by bushes.

After a quick rest break they would then be heading off for the safe haven of Saint Petersburg. Fortunately, by leaving the main highway and using the many other smaller side-roads they'd managed, so far, to avoid any police checks or military road-blocks.

The driver of the first cargo truck, Kostya Liochka, reached across and opened the vehicle's large glove compartment then pulled out a plastic food container inside of which there were several slices of thick, black unbuttered bread and a hunk of evil smelling yellow cheese.

Pulling a wicked looking knife from her waistband, Kostya carved a slice of cheese from the lump, placed it between two slices of black bread, then started chomping it. Noticing her two passengers watching her, she smiled and offered Ed and Captain Zoranski a piece of the ripe smelling cheese.

The Captain shook his head, *"Thank you, Kostya, but not for me."* What Zaronski really needed was a stiff drink, not a piece of honking cheese. Ed graciously accepted a piece of cheese, saying, *"Thanks, Kostya, that's just what I need to keep my strength up!"* and then sat there merrily munching on the cheese. The cheese was very chewy and tasted like wet card-board, but Ed had eaten much worse in his time.

The inside of the hot cab stank of fuel and sweaty bodies. Now the smell of rancid cheese added to the heady brew, making Zoranski feel decidely queasy; his mouth tasting like the bottom of a budgie's cage. As he sat there licking his dry lips, an inconsequential thought flitted through his mind, *"How does anyone know what the bottom of a budgie's cage tastes like?"*

"So, what next, Ed?" asked Zoranski. Ed glanced at his watch and said, *"Well, it'll soon be daylight. We'll wait until the flow of traffic picks up then just filter into it and head straight for my Saint Petersburg contact's place, via*

these back-roads. It'll take a bit longer than using the main highway, but we'll be much safer."

"Might I ask who your contact in Saint Petersburg is?" said Zoranski. Ed shook his head and said, *"Can't tell you that until we get there, my friend. If we have the misfortune to get pulled in by the authorities I want to be one of only a few people that knows my contact's name."*

"Your drivers must know it, surely?" asked Zoranski. *"Yes, they do, but then I trust them not to 'spill the beans.' Don't worry about it, my friend. You'll be one of the first to be introduced to my contact when we arrive at the compound."*

"Fair enough," sighed Zoranski, *"I just hope that you can trust your Saint Petersburg person because it looks like he - or she - is all we've got left now. All of Russia will be out searching for us."*

"Oh, you can trust him - or her - alright. We've worked together for very many years now. In fact we're more like family than business associates," said Ed.

Kostya suddenly yawned, stretched, cocked her buttock cheek and released a thunderous and rather smelly fart before, saying, *"Better out than in, eh, chentlemen!"* stuffing what was left of the bread and cheese inside the plastic container and placing it back inside the truck's glove compartment, much to Captain Zoranski's relief. *"I'll finish that off later,"* she said. Not wishing to cause any offence, Zoranski had to fight not to wrinkle his nose.

Reaching for the truck's door handle, Kostya turned to Ed and said, *"I just need to open the bomb doors before we leave."* Ed nodded. She vaulted out of the cab, found a small bush to hide behind then, lowering her jeans, she crouched down to defacate, completely oblivious to anyone that might be watching - and thinking to herself, *"The cheese tastes great, but it goes through me like lead through a goose!"*

"Ah, a girl after my own heart. She would make a good infanteer," said a smiling Zoranski. *"Just wind the window down a bit my friend and let some fresh air inside the cab will you,"* said Ed. *"It might be better to leave the window closed and not let any noxious smells come in!"* said Zoranski, in a rare attempt at humour.

When Kostya had finished her ablutions she did the necessaries then pulled up her jeans and meandered back to the truck. Jumping back inside the cab she eased herself into the driving seat, grinned and said enthusiastically, *"Right, I'm good to go, Ed!"*

"OK Kostya, better crank up the engine then and let's get moving," said Ed. Kostya nodded and started the truck's engine. She tapped her footbrake twice to warn her partner Artyon that they were about to leave the lay-by; he in turn flashed his headlights back at her indicating that he was also ready to hit the trail.

"Just filter into the morning traffic nice and gently, Kostya. Captain Zoranski and I will keep a sharp eye out for police or military road-blocks." Kostya nodded.

"You know the way from here, Kostya?" asked Zoranski. Kostya nodded, *"Yes, I know these roads like the back of my hand. We often vary our routes to avoid the authorities and have used this particular one many times."* replied a grinning Kostya, then raised a bum cheek and farted loudly. She shrugged her shoulders, smiled coquettishly at Zoranski and said, *"Whoops! It's the cheese, sorry!"*

Turning to Ed, Zoranski asked, *"What happens if we do spot the cops or come across a military road-block, Ed?"*

"If we can't divert or get off the road in time, we'll just have to smash our way through, then drive like bats out of hell and head for the outskirts of Saint Petersburg, using a pre-arranged alternative series of emergency routes." said Ed.

Kostya slapped Zoranski on the shoulder, *"Don't worry my friend, we have done this sort of journey many times before!"* *"Not carring 26 billion stolen dollars and with half of Russia chasing you, you haven't!"* said Zoranski.

"We love a challenge," said a smiling Kostya.

"It's certainly a challenge. The entire Russian Army and the FSB will be out searching for us by now, not to mention the bloody musor (police)," grumbled Zoranski as he peeked into the rear-view mirror.

Zoranski's would willingly have committed murder to get just a sip of vodka. He licked his lips and shivered involuntarily when he thought about how it had been such a very close call escaping from the compound, with 'Chiller' Chelpinsky hot on their heels. Chelpinsky was the spectre at the feast.

Noting his concern, Ed said, *"Don't worry, my friend, they don't really know what our trucks look like. Don't forget, as soon as we arrived at the compound we hid inside the hangar and then left there in the dark. There'll be many other very similar trucks to ours out on the roads today."*

Smiling, he put his arm around Zaronski's shoulders, *"We'll be OK. Artyom and Kostya have done this particular run a thousand times before and know these roads well. I have every faith in their expertise."*

"It'll be daylight before too much longer," said a gloomy Zoranski, *"and then we'll stand no chance of evading capture; along with everything else, they'll have choppers out searching for us,"* he sighed, *"we have wasted far too much time here!"*

"Easy, Tiger," said Ed, *"it won't do any of us any good if Kostya here falls asleep at the wheel, will it. She and Artyom needed a bit of a rest. Don't forget, they've been on the go since yesterday morning without a decent break!"* *"Hey, I do not do flakeys, Ed!"* said a bristling Kostya, *"I can do this drive with my eyes closed!"* *"That's precisely why we stopped for a break,"* said Ed, smiling.

She rammed the gear lever into the gate, revved the engine and then eased her truck out of the lay-by and back onto the road, followed closely by Artyom. The volume of traffic had certainly increased and the road was much busier.

Ed sat back and thought about his contact in Saint Petersburg, a certain Mr Kassim Bishara of 'KASSIM BISHARA IMPORT/EXPORTS.'

Kassim was a likeable rogue who was superb at what he did best - smuggling, although his cover was the legal exporting and importing of fruit, vegetables and furniture to and from various markets throughout Europe. Ed's friend Kassim Bishara was a wealthy, experienced and successful 'Ducker and Diver' who wouldn't have looked out of place trading down London's Petticoat Lane

Ed had pre-warned Kassim that the Moscow airport job was the 'big one' and that his team would be hot-footing it into Saint Petersburg immediately after the robbery, probably just one step ahead of the authorities.

Kassim had laughed heartily, slapped Ed on the back, told him not to worry and said that he would pull out all of the usual stops for him. Ed knew that he could trust Kassim implicitly.

They'd both made a great deal of money together from their smuggling activities - and that was long before Ed's very profitable 'Time-Travel' shenanigans with Mike and Graham.

The massive, bustling port of Saint Petersburg, located in the eastern part of the Gulf of Finland on the Baltic Sea, is known as being one of the world's most popular cruise liner destinations and is also supported by a thriving and profitable cargo trade. It is busy 24 hours a day.

One of the the largest industrial and transport centres in Russia - it was a complex and difficult area to police. It provided a perfect habitat for Kassim and his illegal activities.

'KASSIM BASHARA IMPORT/EXPORTS' had been operating out of the port for very many years and during that time Kassim had established many valuable local contacts in order to make life easier and simpler for him, particularly whenever the complex Russian trading rules required 'bending' a little.

As a young man, Kassim had started off relatively small-time, using just a large shed and an old Russian ex-Army truck whose exhaust pipe belched more fumes than a mill chimney, but now through dint of hard work, he was a major player and a very wealthy man, owning several large, modern buildings and with a fleet of modern vehicles at his disposal.

Over the years, Kassim had lined a lot of influential people's pockets, including several Police and Customs and Excise officials, all key players. Kassim was a very naughty boy.

Tragically, Kassim's only son and heir, Nassim Bashara, had been killed in a firefight with the Taliban whilst doing his statutory stint of national service with the Russian

Armed Forces in Afghanistan. It was there in Afghanistan that Nassim had bumped into and made friends with Ed De Jong. Ed had been up to mischief elsewhere when the Afghanistani fire-fight had taken place but had heard about it soon afterwards.

On his eventual return from Afghanistan, Ed had made a point of visiting Kassim Bashara to pass on his condolences and return to him what remained of his son's personal effects. As a result of that kind gesture, Kassim and Ed became good friends and eventually, recognising that they were both bandits, trusted 'business' partners.

ЖК

CHAPTER NINE

'THE SAINT PETERSBURG COMPOUND'

Inside the large fenced-off compound at Saint Petersburg, Kassim glanced at his expensive gold watch then called out to the powerfully built man guarding the solid metal gates leading into the compound. *"Unlock the gates, cousin, the two trucks will be arriving here very shortly."*

His cousin nodded and started unbolting the heavy metal double gates, getting them ready to swing open.

After about ten minutes there was the distinct growling of truck engines confirming that the vehicles were approaching. Kassim smiled with relief, at last Ed's team were finally arriving in the two URAL-4320 cargo trucks, exactly as planned.

Miraculously they'd managed to avoid any police or military checks on their long flog from Moscow, although they'd only just managed to body-swerve one major road-block by the skin of their teeth, just as it was being set up on both sides of the highway leading into and out of Saint Petersburg. A close call.

As the trucks swung into the compound, Kassim was surprised to spot Ed sat in the passenger seat of the leading truck and wondered what he was doing there. It definitely hadn't been part of the plan that Ed that had so carefully outlined to him.

Something untoward must have happened to have caused Ed to remain with the trucks, he thought. Kassim waved to Ed, who smiled and gave him a very confident 'thumbs-up' sign.

Kassim's gate-guardian had waved the two trucks in then quickly closed and rebolted the gates. Kassim pointed towards a large enclosed shed where the trucks were to be parked up and unloaded.

Artyom and Kostya manoeuvered the trucks expertly into the shed and the shed doors were quickly closed behind them. No-one, as far as Kassim was concerned, had seen the small convoy arriving, so at least that part of the plan had worked very well.

Although it was normal to see vehicles entering and exiting Kassim's compound, it was fairly unusual at that particular time of the day. Kassim realised that in view of the truck's 'hot' contents, they'd better get a move on with the unloading. Time was now of the very essence.

Kassim knew that it was a foregone conclusion that someone in authority, probably the local Police, would come sniffing around the area, certainly over the next few days, and he wanted no evidence left there of either the trucks, the contents of the trucks - or their passengers, when they did.

Ж

CHAPTER TEN

'ESCAPE AND EVASION'

"Right, my dear friends," said Kassim Bishara, *"permit me to explain to you precisely how I plan to get you and your dollars safely out of Saint Petersburg. It isn't going to be easy, I hear through the grapevine that already you've stirred up quite a hornets nest between here and Moscow!"*

"It was only to be expected, Kassim, especially when we've relieved the top man's friend of many millions of dollars," said Ed.

Kassim smiled and nodded in agreement, then continued, *"This is what will happen. My cousin, who you saw earlier, will continue to man the main gate here and has orders to keep an eye out for any suspicious activity or unexpected arrivals,"* said Kassim.

"The gates, sturdy as they are, would not be able prevent anyone from forcing their way inside the compound, particularly as the security forces will be very determined to get in here and have a nose around should they arrive here. It's what they do best. They are like shit-house rats."

"We'd better get cracking then," said Ed.

"Don't worry, my friend," said Kassim, winking, *"I've got several of my people out on the streets keeping a watchful eye on things for us. We'll soon be warned off if anything unusual is taking place."*

A more serious looking Kassim continued *"I have made arrangements to get you out of here and off to an alternative safe location at very short notice, if required, and this is how we will proceed."*

"As we know Ed, your two boys have already left here and are travelling overland by hire car to Helsinki. They should be able to do that without any problem, especially if they're anything like their father!" he added, with a smile.

"As for the four of you key players; tomorrow morning at 0900 hours you will leave here in my cousin's boat-taxi along the Neva River andbe ferried right into central Saint Petersburg."

'Church of the Savior of Spilled Blood'
Saint Petersburg

"My cousin has been instructed to drop you off close to the 'Church of the Savior on Spilled Blood,' which will be jam-packed with tourists and tourist buses at that time of day. It always is, so we will all be able to blend in quite easily." A puzzled Ed looked at Kassim and asked, *"You said – we, Kassim?"*

Kassim nodded, *"That is correct, my friend. I said 'we' Ed, because I have decided that I am going to go with you and will escort you personally to 'Touristik Bus' Number 19, which another of my cousin's will be driving."*

"You've got an awful lot of cousins, Kassim," said Mike. Kassim grinned and winked, *"We are all good Catholics in my family, Mike!"* he said, then continued, *"I then plan to hand you over to my bus driving cousin who has agreed to take you to the Saint Petersburg Port Terminal."*

"Not coming to the Port with us then, Kassim?" asked Graham. Kassim shook his head. *"No, my friend. Once you are safely on board the bus and have departed from the church parking zone, I will be returning home by a completely different route."*

Kassim continued, *"My cousin's Touristik bus travels backwards and forwards between the centre of Saint Petersburg and the Port Terminal throughout the day, so there's always plenty of tourists getting on and off it, which will give you plenty of cover should anyone be watching."*

"Please remember though, that my cousin will be accompanied throughout by an official State Bus Escort. Once you have boarded the bus, you must be very careful what you say and how you behave. State Bus Escorts are a standing requirement of our Security Services and they are put there to closely monitor everything that is going on."

"They are trained to hear and see everything, and will report anything unusual or suspicious back to their FSB masters. They are like shit-house rats."

"You'll also be pleased to know that I have obtained some pretty circular numbered stickers of the type that tourists wear, for you to attach to your clothing. They will help to allay the State Bus Escort's suspicions. You must board the bus exhuding confidence and look as if you had every right to be there."

"And what happens once we reach the Port Terminal, Kassim?" asked Graham, *"When me and Mike passed through there a couple of years ago on a leisure cruise, if memory serves, we had to carry our Passports and a current Russian Tourist Visa with us at all times? It was a right old faff as I recall. Remember that Mike?!"*

Mike nodded, *"Aye, that's right, we were asked to produce them for inspection several times - and remember those bloody queues of tourists waiting to get back inside the Port Terminal, Graham? They went on for miles."*

Graham nodded, *"Aye, there were more cruise ships in the harbour that day than we Brits used at the relief of Dunkirk!"*

'The busy Port Terminal at Saint Petersburg'

Kassim nodded then added reassuringly, *"Yes, well of course this is Russia and you can't fart out of tune here without having written authority. Although that is normally the case, we are not 'normal' people are we, my friend."*

"You have absolutely no cause for concern, gentlemen, you are about to become part of a tried and tested well-oiled operation, one that my organisation has used successfully on many occasions."

Kassim continued**,** *"Now, once you arrive at the Port Terminal you must exit the Touristik bus, mingle with the rest of the tourists, then head straight to the main terminal entrance where you will see a sign pointing to the men's toilets."*

"*Waiting underneath the Finnlandia Shipping Line sign near the toilets will be a cousin of mine,*" he smiled, "*yes, another one! She will be wearing a dark blue uniform with an easily recognisable Finnlandia Shipping Line badge pinned onto her lapel with her name prominently displayed on it.*"

"*Her name is Galina Restikov - she'll be holding a clip-board and doing her best to look important. Nobody ever questions anyone holding a clip-board do they!*"

The lads smiled and nodded in agreement.

Kassim continued, "*Galina is expecting you, so make yourselves known to her. Just say my name quietly, and then she will then take you away to a side office which leads into the port terminal complex itself. Galina will escort you through to the dockside where the ship, the 'MV Solar Star' is berthed.*"

"*They know that you are coming, so you can go straight on board. The Captain of the ship ...*" "*Your cousin?*" asked Mike. Kassim shook his head, "*My cousin's son, is also expecting you!*" They all laughed.

"*The Captain of the 'MV Solar Star,'*" said Kassim, "*has done a lot of this type of work for me over the years and is a man of honour. You will be perfectly safe in his hands.*"

Kassim continued, "*Several key people inside the complex have been paid to look the other way as you pass through* there. We always use a route that cleverly avoids the all-invasive electronic surveillance equipment. It is a slick procedure that we have used successfully on many other occasions and one that has not failed us yet."

"Once safely on-board the 'MV Solar Star' you will be taken straight to your cabins and must remain there, out of sight, until you are well out into the Gulf of Finland and the safety of international waters. Only then will you be away from the immediate clutches of the Russian authorities," said Kassim. "OK so far, gentlemen?" asked Kassim.

Mike, Ed, Graham and Captain Zoranski all nodded.

"You will be sailing from Saint Petersburg directly to Helsinki. On arrival at Helsinki, the Captain has arranged to get you ashore without having to pass through Customs. I have assumed that you will be able to make your own arrangements for travelling onwards from there?" he said looking across at Ed.

Ed nodded, "That won't be a problem, Kassim," he said confidently, "Deiderik and Ludo will meet up with us at Helsinki, after which both the cargo containers and my boys will transfer to the 'MV Europe Oceana' which will then be sailing on to the Port of Rotterdam."

"Meanwhile, in Helsinki we'll get a hire car from Hertz, then me, Graham, Mike and good old Captain Zoranski here can drive overland to the Netherlands. It'll be a long flog, but if we're careful and stick to the routes that I'm *familiar with, we shouldn't need to produce any sort of travel documentation. As you know, Kassim, border crossings are my speciality."* Kassim smiled, *"You are like the Scarlet Pimpernel, my friend!"*

"If we get our collective clogs down," Ed continued, *"we'll be home long before the 'MV Europe Oceana' docks in the Port of Rotterdam and can meet up there with the lads - and the containers to supervise the move to Amsterdam. That's the bones of the plan anyway,"* said Ed.

"It's such a damned travesty that the 'T3-Travellator' was shot to pieces by that bloody dozy Russian Sergeant," said Mike, *"we'll all have saddle-sores by the time we reach Amsterdam thanks to him!"*

"Oh, cheer up Mike, it'll be a cracking trip and we'll be able to do a bit of sight-seeing along the way," said Graham. *"Aye, well let's make sure that we hire a decent car in Helsinki, Ed. A nice comfy Merc, or a BMW, something like that,"* said Mike, *"not one of your wee Japanese biscuit tins, or even worse, a clunky bloody Volvo!"*

"Just as a matter of interest Ed," asked Graham, *" what's happening to those two brilliant drivers of yours, Artyom and Kostya?"*

Ed replied, *"Oh, don't worry about those two bandits, they're 'Old South China Sea Hands.' They've made their* own *'dispersal'* arrangements. *In fact they're well on their way home as we speak."*

"Home being where?" asked Mike. *"Somewhere unpronounceable in Latvia. They're well used to dropping off the radar - you won't be seeing them again,"* replied Ed.

Kassim added, *"The two URAL-4320 cargo trucks have now been unloaded and are being taken to a local scrapyard for dissembling. The remains of the trucks will be disposed of before the day is out. Any evidence of them will have totally disappeared; meaning that there'll be nothing left to link them to us. No cargo, no trucks, no drivers,"* said Kassim.

"Shame that, they were very reliable vehicles, but it's better to be safe than sorry," said Ed.

"Hope that your scrap-dealer contact can be trusted, you know what scrappies are like!" said Graham. Kassim smiled and replied, *"Ah my dear friend, that will not be a problem. I own that particular scrap-yard, although I'm a silent partner. The Manager is ....!"*

Mike and Graham both said at the same time, *"Another cousin?"* Kassim nodded, winked and said, *"Is the Pope a Catholic!"* *"His Holiness is probably your cousin as well!"* said Graham.

A laughing Kassim continued, *"Now, His Holiness would be a good contact! Anyway, enough plotting and scheming for now, let's go and find something to eat. My stomach's beginning to think that my throat's been cut. After we've eaten we can talk through the 'Escape and Evasion' plans more thoroughly."*

Graham asked, *"Do they do a 'full English' in Saint Petersburg, Kassim?"* *"Don't you mean a 'full Scottish!"* said Mike, *"Or maybe even a 'full Russian'?"* said Ed. *"I dinnae eat horse-meat,"* said Mike.

Ж

CHAPTER ELEVEN

'HEADING FOR HOME'

As previously promised by Kassim, the team's arrival and 'processing' through the very busy Port Terminal at Saint Petersburg the following day, although nerve-twanging, went like a well-oiled dream.

Ed, Graham, Mike and Rostislav Zoranski, (now called Rosti by everyone – to save time), had experienced no difficulty whatsoever on the Tourist Bus. The driver had been expecting them and made sure that they sat near to the central doors of the bus so that they could exit with ease.

Kassim's cousin, the confident and mega-efficient Galina Restikov met them near the 'facilities' exactly as planned and had escorted them directly through to the cargo ship, the 'MV Solar Star.' They weren't stopped nor were they asked to provide any identification.

A rapidly sobering Rosti thought that not only was Galina confident and efficient, she was very easy on the eye. He asked for, and to his surprise, got her telephone number. The less vodka Zoranski drank, the more he realised just what he'd been missing out on by being pissed out of his skull throughout each day.

The transfer from 'port to ship' was slick and obviously well practised. Ed, and his team, along with their new friend Rosti Zoranski, who had now dispensed with his Army uniform and been kitted out with nondescript casual civilian clothing, had boarded the ship without any difficulty whatsoever and been directed to two roomy and relatively well-appointed cabins. The cabins weren't of the same standard as the staterooms on tourist ships like the 'Royal Caribbean' line, but nevertheless were passable - bordering on comfortable.

Much to Rosti's delight, they'd been provided with a large well stacked drinks tray and a bucket of ice in each cabin. Although he'd not touched alcohol since arriving in Kassim's compound, so as far as Zoranski was concerned, things were definitely looking up. Having said that, rather sensibly he'd decided not to overdo things as they still weren't quite out of the woods yet and he wanted to keep his wits about him.

They'd sailed out of the Port of Saint Petersburg and much to everyone's relief were well out into international waters, steaming towards Helsinki, before you could say 'Nikita Khruschev.'

Kassim's relative, the ship's Captain, had very kindly agreed to radio on ahead and arrange for a quality hire car, a fully fuelled Mercedes Benz Estate, to be parked up just inside the Helsinki port entrance, waiting for Ed to collect the keys. All Ed and his team had to do was disembark, transfer to the car and then 'leg it' for the border.

At the port in Helsinki, Ed's two sons, Deiderick and Ludo would board the 'MV Europe Oceana,' remaining with the ship until it arrived at the Port of Rotterdam, taking it in turns to keep a watchful eye on the two valuable cargo containers for the duration of the journey.

Shortly after weighing anchor and the 'MV Solar Star' clearing the Port of Saint Petersburg, the ship's Captain had popped down from the bridge to Ed's cabin to introduce himself, say a quick hello and check that everything was alright.

The Captain had informed Ed about their hire car reservation and explained that he'd made arrangements for Ed and his team to be able to exit the Port of Helsinki without any problems from the authorities, shortly after the ship had docked.

Naturally, money had changed hands to achieve that, but Kassim had seen to everything. It was all that simple.

Kassim Bashara's organisation had ensured that the two all-important metal cargo containers containing the stolen dollars had arrived safely at the 'MV Solar Star' and had been craned aboard, then secured to the deck. Immediately after the containers had been chained down, the ship cast off.

The initial problem, getting the men and the cargo containers out of Russia, had been resolved. Surprisingly, the Russian Port Authorities had cleared the ship and its cargo without any problems and they'd left Russian waters with consummate ease and were now heading safely through international waters.

For the moment, anyway, things were going exactly to plan.

Ж

CHAPTER TWELVE

'ALL IS SAFELY GATHERED IN'

Ed, Mike, Graham and Rosti Zoranski had eventually arrived safely in Amsterdam after a long, boring but uneventful flog by road from Finland. The journey overland had seemed to drag on interminably, although Graham, who loved travelling, had lapped it up.

The drive, some 2,700+ kilometres, had been tiring, but as they'd all taken turns behind the wheel, (including Rosti - who had sobered up and was, surprisingly, turning into quite a personable individual), so the lengthy journey hadn't been as exhausting as it might have been.

At first Ed had considered it unwise to let Rosti drive as he thought that he'd still have too much vodka in his system. Rosti, however, had convinced Ed that he was perfectly capable, so Ed changed his mind and decided to trust him to take a turn at the wheel. Rosti hadn't let him down.

Unsurprisingly, Ed De Jong had many contacts en route and made full use of them to help by-pass various border and customs posts and any other form of officialdom. They'd even kept to the official speed limits throughout the drive so as not to attract any unwanted attention from the traffic police.

The only problem they'd had was Mike's constant complaints about his back feeling like, "*A twisted crisp!*" Graham told him to stop wittering and loosen his money belt by a few notches. They were all greatly relieved when finally arriving safe and sound at Ed's place in Amsterdam.

Shortly after they got there, their hire car was collected by one of Ed's men and driven off to Düsseldorf Airport in Germany for handing back to the Hertz International Car-hire firm. The last thing Ed wanted was for the Russians to be able to trace the vehicle back to Amsterdam.

Much to everyone's relief, the cargo containers had also arrived safely in the Port of Rotterdam on board the 'MV Europe Oceana.' Ed's two sons, Deidrick and Ludo had kept a watchful eye on all of the arrangements for the transferring of the two cargo containers from the 'MV Solar Star' during the change-over in Helsinki.

All that was required now was the unloading and safe onwards transmission of the two containers to Ed's ultra-secure compound in Amsterdam, where they would be tucked away out of sight and then their precious cargo unloaded ready for disposal.

Ed and his team were stood waiting at the dockside in Rotterdam to ensure that everything went without a hitch, which it did.

Ed, Mike, Graham and a now fully sober Rosti Zoranski were sat drinking coffee in Ed's Rotterdam office. *"So, now that we've done the difficult bit, where do we go from here then, Ed?"* asked Mike. *"In what respect?"* said Ed.

"Well, without going into the complete administrative minutiae, have you decided how we're going to dispose of all that filthy lucre out there?" said Mike, pointing towards the corner of the compound where the two cargo containers were safely tucked out of harms away.

"Naturally, I've given the matter a great deal of thought," said Ed, *"and I have the following suggestion to make to you all regarding how we should distribute our ill-gotten gains."*

He went on to outline his suggestions:

a.   **$20 billion dollars to go back to the Iraqi's.**

"After all" said Ed, *"the money was theirs to begin with. The Iraqi's have a Consulate General's office here in Amsterdam. I can contact a friend of mine who works there as Trade Secretary and make the necessary transfer arrangements, once we all agree to it, that is."*

b.   **Then $2 billion to go to the Americans.**

"Who'll probably snap our hands off and fly the money straight out of Schiphol Airport quicker than you can say Donald Trump."

c.   And finally, $2 billion to go to your beloved UK government.

"Aye, well knowing that bloody useless shower in the English Parliament, they'll probably send it out tae Iraq as Foreign Aid anyway," said Mike.

"We're not too bothered what they do with it, are we, boys and girls," said Graham, *"I mean, it's not as if any of it was our dosh in the first place."*

Ed continued:

d.   And last, but not least, we keep the princely sum of $2 billion dollars, for ourselves.

"Aye, well I suppose that's a very fair distribution of wealth, given the circumstances," said Mike.

"Everyone's in agreement then?" asked Ed. They all nodded their approval.

"Incidentally, Ed, what about our mate Kassim Bashara and his family?" asked Mike. *"That's already been taken care of,"* replied Ed, *"Kassim's was more than happy with what I paid him, which I might add was very generous - and we can deduct that amount from our $2 billion without it even causing a dent. So, are we all in agreement then?"*

Everyone nodded their agreement.

Mike asked, "*Incidentally, what's $2 billion divided by five then, Ed?*" "*$400 million each, give or take a few cents here and there,*" said Ed. "*Chuffing hell lads, we're pigging loaded!*" said a highly elated Graham, "*I feel a Bentley coming on!*"

"*Hang on a moment though,*" said Ed, "*it's not divided by five is it; it's divided by six. We mustn't forget good old Rosti here. Without his help we couldn't have done it!*"

"*Bugger it, that reduces the money to only $333 million or so dollars each. How on earth are we expected to scrape by on that!*" said Mike. They all laughed, including Rosti.

Ed continued, "*So Graham, if you could get on to your government contacts back in the UK and have them put arrangements in train regarding the collection of their $2 billion, that would be great. The sooner we get it away from here the better, particularly as the Russian FSB will be rampaging around doing their utmost trying to recover it.*"

Graham nodded, "*Right Ed, I'll get on to Downing Street straight after this little meeting. They'll snap our hands off, I can guarantee that!*"

"*I've got my guys supervising the splitting up of the dollars in readiness,*" said Ed, "*they should be finished by lunchtime.*" "*It's going to be a long job counting that lot, don't forget that there's 26 pallets, each containing $1 billion dollars,*" said Graham.

Ed smiled, *"Not a problem, old friend. It's simply a matter of counting the contents of the first pallet and then weighing it. All we have to do then is weigh the remainder of the money and put it on the pallets in the amounts that we've just agreed. We might be out by a few dollars here and there, but no-one's going to whinge about that, are they!"*

"So how do you intend 'disposing' of our share, Ed?" asked Graham. *"What, you mean banking it?"* asked Ed. Graham nodded.

"I've already organised for our $2 billion to be transferred to the bank that holds our off-shore accounts via my friendly bank manager here in Rotterdam. Once there it will be sub-divided and stashed away in each of our personal bank accounts."

A grinning Mike rubbed his hands together, *"Och, all those bundles of lovely, crisp green-backs just sat there safe and sound in the bank vaults accruing interest. I cannae believe it! All of my Christmases have come at once. I feel a wee dram coming on!"*

"Right," said Graham, *"well I'd better go and make that 'phone call to Downing Street before I get overcome with excitement."*

Later, when he'd returned, Graham said, *"OK chaps, I've just finished speaking to the Prime Minister's Chief of Staff. Needless to say, he was over the moon. Talk about striking whilst the iron's hot. If we can, he'd like us to arrange for the money to be shipped across to Hull by P & O Ferries as soon as possible, using one of our cargo containers, where it'll then be collected by an armed detachment from a local army unit and then be trucked down to London with a police escort."*

Ed nodded, *"That won't be a problem. I'll get on to my guys at the ferry terminal to get that organised straight away."*

Graham continued, *"The PM, apparently, is chuffed to bits and said that the money's come just at the right moment. He's going to use most of it to give the NHS a bit of a boost." "Not before bloody time!"* growled Mike.

"OK," said Ed, *"I've put out feelers to a friend of mine who's an Iraqi Trade Secretary called Telenaz Hikmat. He actually lives here in Amsterdam. I asked him to scope out arrangements for the collection of the Iraqi share of the money, asap."*

"He's going to arrange to have it loaded onto an Iraqi vessel, the 'MV Chama Globtik,' which is run by the Shiref Shipping Company. It sails tomorrow morning for a place called Khor Al Zubair in Iraq."

"Telenaz is arranging for a truck to come here late this evening to pick up the loot and haul it away. I've told him that he can have one of the cargo containers. Again, we need to get it shifted out of these premises fairly rapidly and before the Russians get wind of what we're up to."

"And what about the American share?" asked Graham.

"I've also spoken to my American contact who has an office here in Amsterdam," said Ed, *"He told me that they'll send a vehicle here this evening to take away their $2 billion."*

"They'll be bringing their own container and once we've got the money loaded onto their truck it'll be driven to Schiphol Airport to be transferred onto a USAF cargo aircraft which will be leaving for the USA, via Mildenhall, at midnight tonight."

"So that's the Brit, Yank and Iraqi side of things sorted out." "My God, you've been busy, Ed, " said Mike.

Ed smiled, *"Well, it's not been as complicated as it sounds, not when you're as used to moving illicit loads around the planet for as many years as I have - and have as many useful contacts as I do,"* he said. Graham shook his head in wonderment and murmured *"It's a different world, cocker."*

Ed looked at across at Rostislav, *"Rosti, I've also sorted out your new passport, your visa and paperwork, and have booked you on a flight out of here. I've been assured that there won't be any problems at either the Schipol or Canadian end, my friend."*

Rostislav grinned, *"Good, that is good. I want to be well out of the way before the FSB get wind of anything. Their testicles are everywhere.*" Graham smiled and said, "*I think you mean tentacles, Rosti!*" Everyone laughed.

Ж

CHAPTER THIRTEEN

'THE BREAK-THROUGH'

"At long last, the all-important break-through that we have been waiting for, Comrade General," said a greatly relieved Colonel Ivanski Gregorovitch. *"Out with it man - what news have we?"* snapped General Chelpinski, stubbing his foul smelling cheroot out in the overflowing ash-tray.

"Well sir, our man in Saint Petersburg, who is in contact with an employee who works in a large scrap-yard on the outskirts of the city, has had it reported to him that two trucks, similar to the ones we have been searching for, the URAL-4320's, were delivered to the yard with instructions for them to be dismantled, the remnants crushed beyond recognition and then disposed of. He stated that the trucks were quite empty when they arrived at the scrap-yard."

For the first time in two days, something resembling a smile flitted across General Chelpinski's haggard face, *"Yes, but how do we know that they are the same two truck's we've been searching for, Ivanski?"* he asked.

"Because, sir, the man involved with sending the trucks to the scrap-dealer is a reprobate called Kassim Bashara, who is well-known to the local police for his smuggling, thieving and various other criminal activities. It is too much of a coincidence to ignore."

General Chelpinski nodded, *"I agree. Mmm, this man Bashara would not want the trucks, valuable assets to him presumably, disposing of - unless he had something to hide. Taking everything into consideration, you are quite right Ivanski, it is too much of a coincidence and as you know, I don't believe in coincidence."*

Ivanski was greatly relieved. His General and mentor needed news like this to raise his spirits and cheer him up. The Russian President was having Chelpinski's every move closely monitored. The threat of demotion dangled over the General's head like the 'Sword of Damocles.'

"Do we know who was it that delivered the trucks to the scrap-yard?" the General asked.

"Two family members of this man Kassim Bashara, General. Bashara is a local 'wheeler dealer' who has been the owner of a Saint Petersburg licensed Import/Export firm in the city for many years. He involves all of his family in his illegal activities," said Colonel Gregorovitch, hurriedly reading through his notes.

He continued, *"I spoke to the local Police Chief who told me that he has long suspected Bashara of being up to all sorts of mischief, but said that he was as slippery as an eel and could never pin anything on him."*

Chelpinski snorted, *"How ridiculous! Since when have we needed evidence to pin something on someone, eh? I take it that we now have Bashara in custody?"* he asked.

Ivanski nodded, *"Yes sir, he was caught attempting to escape from his compound hiding in the boot of a car, but we had the entire place surrounded, so there was nowhere for him to go."*

"And who is the local Police Chief?" asked Chelpinski. Gregorovitch examined the notes that were pinned to his clip-board, *"He is, now let me see, are here we are, Police Commissioner Dimitri Fyodor Gennadski, sir. He has been in post there for several years."* *"Obviously for several years too long!"* said Chelpinsky.

After a few moments deep in thought, Chelpinski continued, *"Arrest Gennadski then have both him and Bashara brought here to Moscow immediately for questioning. If Police Commissioner Gennadski claims that he has been unable to sort out a mere 'wheeler dealer' then he is a weak man who at the very least has had his nose in the trough. Have him pulled in using my Presidential authority."*

Gregorovitch nodded, *"Very well, sir."*

Chelpinsky continued, *"This man Kassim Bashara obviously didn't carry out this robbery all by himself, so what about the others that were involved,"* he asked, *"and more importantly, Ivanski, what about the money? Where the hell is it now? And as for the thief, Captain Zoranski, once he is brought to book, I want something very special organised for his 'departure' from this world, once we've finished with what's left of him, that is."*

A grim faced Chelpinski continued, *"I would like to deal with Zoranski's final interrogation myself, after which, if he survives the experience, he is to be taken down to the Furnace Room for disposal. Does Zoranski have any living relatives?" "Just one, an ancient Aunt who lives on the outskirts of Moscow, sir"* said Gregorovitch.

"Have the old fart pulled in," said Chelpinsky, *"she can take a short drop too."*

"We have been 'working' on Bashara since his arrest, Comrade General. Not much information forthcoming as yet, he's a tough cookie, but he'll cough up everything we need to know, eventually," said Gregorovitch.

General Chelpinsky nodded and smiled knowingly, *"Yes, they always do, don't they. Tell his interrogators to save something for me to do. I like to try and keep my hand in!"*

Ivanski nodded and continued, *"I will inform them, General. What we have also discovered from our Saint Petersburg FSB office is that on the day the two URAL-4320 trucks were sent to the scrap-yard, two large metal containers left Kassim Bashara's premises and were delivered to the docks at Saint Petersburg, where they were then loaded onto a cargo ship,"* he checked his clipboard again, *"the 'MV Solar Star.'"*

"And let me guess, Ivanski, the 'MV Solar Star' has sailed from Saint Petersburg?" Gregorovitch nodded, *"I'm afraid so, Comrade General. It is in international waters and well on its way to Helsinki as we speak."*

"Ye-bat!" shouted Chelpinski, using a very rude Russian swear word, slamming his hand on the desk in front of him, *"Can we not have it stopped, turned around and brought back to port, and the money recovered - because that's obviously where it is - inside those two damned shipping containers!"*

Igor shook his head, *"I'm afraid not, General. By the time we got the information, the ship had cleared the port and was well out into international waters,"* he looked at his watch, *"in fact it will be docking in Helsinki in approximately seven hours, possibly making it too late for us to arrange anything at the Helsinki end."*

Chelpinski was furious, *"I'll have someone's balls in a vice for this, Ivanski. Find out how those two cargo containers got through to the port without being checked properly. We're supposed to have everything closed down and tight as a duck's arse! It's either been an act of bloody gross inefficiency or it's more than likely that someone has got their finger in the pie, if you ask me!"*

Gregorovitch nodded, *"We don't quite know how they did it, yet, but they definitely managed to slip the containers through the dragnet, Comrade General,"* said Colonel Gregorovitch.

"We need to find out about the rest of the team involved in the robbery, Ivanski," said Chelpinski, *"Who are they? What has happened to them? Where are they? They can't just have vanished into thin air! That man Bashara knows something about it! He must be made to speak, and quickly!"*

Chelpinski sat back, sighed, and then rubbed his forehead, *"Oh no, I think I'm getting another of my headaches."*

Reaching into his desk for some aspirins, Chelpinski then ordered, *"I want Bashara and the ex-Saint Petersburg Police Commissioner flown here to Moscow immediately! Send a military helicopter for them if necessary. I will personally find out what has gone on in Saint Petersburg and also what those bandits have planned for Helsinki! Get me a glass of vodka to wash these tablets down with will you, Ivanski."*

Pouring the General a glass of vodka, a nodding Colonel Gregorovitch replied, *"If I might have your permission to use the 'Priority Red' telephone to get things moving, it would save a great deal of invaluable time, Comrade General?"*

Chelpinski nodded, *"Yes of course, Ivanski. Just get on with it! Pass me that glass of vodka first though."* The General tossed two aspirins into his mouth then washed them down his throat with the vodka. He held the glass out, *"And another one for luck please, Ivanski."*

The large ornate ormolu clock, a war trophy filched by the Russian army from Hitler's Bunker near the Berlin Reichstag at the end of World War 2, was ticking away quietly but relentlessly on a small desk in a corner of the Russian President's office.

The clock, which had been Adolf Hitler's pride and joy, was the only thing in there, other than the President himself, that dared to make a noise.

'The French 18th Century Louis the XV Period Clock'

Suddenly, the 'Priority Red' telephone on the President's desk rang, shattering the ominous silence. Baronovski snatched it up and snarled, *"This had better be important!"*

The fearful telephone operator informed the President that there were two calls requiring his attention. One from the President of the United States of America and the other from General Chelpinski, both of whom were waiting on the line, requesting to speak to him.

"Inform Mr Trump that I'll have someone call him back tomorrow, and as for the General, make him wait for precisely five minutes, then put him through to me!" commanded the Russian President, before slamming his 'phone back onto its cradle.

The President reached across his desk, picked up a lead pencil and snapped in half, hurtling the broken pieces across his office. Over in the far corner of his office was a small but ever increasing pile of broken pencils.

The President considered that his job wasn't half as much fun as it had been as when he'd first been 'elected.' Baronovski liked to think that he was a man-of-action and not some 'quill-dribbling' politician tied to a desk, signing meaningless piles of documents all day, every day, which was happening to him with increasing regularity

Precisely five minutes later the President's 'Priority Red' 'phone rang again. He snatched it up and answered it.

"This is the Comrade Supreme Commander speaking," he said. A timid voice replied, *"Good morning, Comrade Supreme Commander, this is…"*

The President interrupted General Chelpinski, *"I know who it is, you imbecile! What news do you have for me - and it had better be good!"* said the sour-faced President, his voice cold as ice.

As he was listening to General Chelpinski, Baronovski glanced across at the wall where a large oil painting of ex-

President Saddam Hussein was hung. Saddam appeared to be glaring down at him almost accusingly. The painting reminded him that his friend Saddam had been most displeased when he'd heard about the robbery from the compound and had made several very caustic comments about the gross inefficiency of the FSB. Baronovsky quickly broke contact with Saddam's piercing eyes.

As he listened to what Chelpinski had to say to him, Baronovski felt a surge of white-hot anger coursing through his body and reached for another pencil to snap. The General was not telling him what he wanted to hear.

Ж

CHAPTER FOURTEEN

'BACK TO IRAQ'

Telenaz Hikmat, was the Trade Secretary at the Iraqi Trade Mission in Amsterdam and also Ed De Jong's contact. Something that Telenaz Hikmat's Iraqi masters didn't know was that he was in fact a long-term double-agent in the pay of the Russians.

He'd been 'inserted' into the Iraqi Diplomatic Service many years ago by the Russians when things were a lot more chaotic in Iraq. Telenaz was a very clever man, but one who continually trod a thin and dangerous line.

Hikmat, an Omar Sharif lookalike, was an erudite, suave operator who always had an eye on the main chance. He also had an eye for the ladies, loved nice cars and liked to have a few dollars tucked away in his hidden bank account - and that's how he'd crossed paths with Ed De Jong.

To maintain the high standards that he kept, Telenaz had been involved in many illicit and financially rewarding deals with Ed, not only that, he liked and trusted Ed. They had become friends, or so Ed believed.

Wearing his 'Russian Spy' hat, Hikmat had recently been on the 'phone speaking to the Russian FSB's Colonel Ivanski Gregorovitch, where he'd explained to Ivanski the precise circumstances of how 20 billion American dollars had come into his possession and the instructions that he'd received from the 'donor' that the money had to be returned to the people of Iraq, to whom it rightfully belonged.

Hikmat had then gone on to explain to Ivanski that the large metal cargo container in which the money was safely stashed away had been collected and loaded onto the Iraqi's Shiref Shipping Lines cargo ship the 'MV Chama Globtik' which had been given clearance to leave the Port of Rotterdam and would be leaving for the Port of Khor al Zubair in Iraq within the next 24 hours.

On arrival in Khor al Zubair the money from the container would be handed over to the Iraqi Secret Service, (the Mukhabarat), for onwards transmission to a bank in central Baghdad. The announcement of the money's pending arrival had caused a great stir in the constantly cash-strapped Iraq.

Ivanski had thanked Telenaz profusely and congratulated him for his good work in obtaining the information. Telenaz was then instructed to stand by to receive further instructions.

Needless to say, Gregorovitch was delighted at the news and very nearly left skid-marks on the floor in his rush to go and tell General Chelpinski.

An hour or so later, Gregorovitch got back to Telenaz, ordered him to secure a berth on board the ship and then set sail with it under the guise of keeping a watchful eye on such an important cargo. He was also told not to worry about seeking permission to do so from the Iraqi Ambassador in the Hague, who was himself in the pay of the Russians. That little bit of news astounded Telenaz who hadn't had an inkling that his Ambassador was as bent as a corkscrew.

Telenaz was also informed that arrangements were being made to have the 'MV Chama Globtik' stopped at sea by the Russian Navy, after which the money would be cross-loaded onto the Russian vessel, where it would then be returned to the Port of Saint Petersburg and thence on to Moscow.

Much to his relief, Telenaz was told that his time as a spy was now at an end and that he was to accompany the cargo container until its contents were transferred onto the Russian vessel; then both he and the money would be taken to Saint Petersburg for handing over to the Security Services, after which he would be welcomed home to Moscow as a hero.

That was good news and a great relief as far as Telenaz was concerned; he'd recently he'd felt that things were closing in on him at work and that it was probably time for him to return home.

The Iraqi Ambassador had recently welcomed a newly appointed and very efficient Security Chief into the Iraqi

Embassy and Telenaz had the distinct feeling that he had been coming under very close scrutiny, which made him feel distinctly uncomfortable. The new man was not a gentleman, in both senses of the word.

The Iraqi Ambassador who lived in his official residence at the Hague, was a thoroughly corrupt and unpleasant individual who, since he had assumed his appointment two years previously had seemed to take great enjoyment out of making life difficult for Telenaz and his small band of loyal and hard-working support staff. The revelation that he was also working for the Russians had shaken Telenaz to the core.

In all honesty, Telenaz was greatly relieved that finally he was being ordered to return home to 'Mother Russia,' having already concluded that it was time for him to retire from the spying game - and that finally he would be able to relax and shave off his much hated beard and drooping moustache.

And how nice it would be for him not to have to be constantly looking over his shoulder, always wondering if the new Iraqi Security Chief was on to him. In the event that his role as a Russian spy been uncovered by the Iraqi Security Services, his treatment at their hands would have been unthinkable. He knew that would be drugged and flown back to Iraq, then tortured and eventually executed, probably in a most cruel manner, so it was high time for him to take his leave.

Meanwhile, back in a chilly Moscow, a delighted General Chelpinski, on hearing of the message passed on by Telenaz Hikmat, (who was in reality Colonel Mikhail Kotov), had ordered Colonel Gregorovitch to, *"Ivanski, get in touch immediately with the Kontradmiral of the Northern Fleet Naval Base at Saint Petersburg and order him to get something - anything that floats - out into the Gulf of Finland ready to intercept and stop the 'MV Chama Globtik.'"*

Gregorovitch was busy scribbling notes as Chelpinski continued, *"He is then to have the ship boarded by our men, who are to locate the cargo container and its contents, recover the President's dollars, which are then to be transferred immediately onto our ship."*

"Oh, and Ivanski, inform the Kontradmiral that there will be a 'special' passenger on board the ship."

"A special passenger, General?" queried Ivanski.

Chelpinski nodded, *"Yes. The passenger is Telenaz Hikmat, or as we know him, Colonel Mikhail Kotov. The Colonel, as you know, has been embedded with the Iraqi's and spying for us for many years and it is now time for him to return home."*

"The Colonel has done way beyond what was expected of him whilst under cover and it is vital, now that his time has drawn to a close, that he be brought safely home to Mother Russia."

"Under no circumstances is he to be left behind on that Iraqi cargo ship. Make that absolutely clear to the Kontradmiral! Mikhail Kotov is one of the good guys and we are duty bound to look after him."

Ivanski nodded, *"I will make sure that the Kontradmiral is fully aware of that, sir."*

An animated Chelpinski continued, *"We must all remain completely focussed on this task until such time as both the money and the man are recovered and brough back home, Ivanski."* he said, *"the money, naturally, being the main priority."*

"Excuse me, General, but what if the Kontradmiral at Saint Petersburg gets, how can I put this, difficult with me?" asked Gregorovitch.

"Difficult? How do you mean 'difficult,' Ivanski?" asked Chelpinski.

"Well, he might very well resist and start pulling rank on me," replied Gregorovitch, *"with the greatest of respect, sir, our Kontradmirals are renown for being a little flinty and obstructive."*

Chelpinsky sighed, *"If he has the temerity to query the order, inform him that we are working under the direct orders of the Comrade Supreme Commander himself. Fax him a copy of the letter of presidential authority if he requires further encouragement to do his duty."*

"If he still refuses to obey, give him my compliments and tell him that I will speak to the President and arrange to have the Kontradmiral reduced in rank before the day is out and I guarantee that he will be posted as far away from the sea as possible. I have neither the time nor the inclination to fart-arse about!"

Gregorovitch smiled, *"I'll get straight onto it, Comrade General,"* then scuttled off to the Central Operations Room.

Looking heavenwards, Chelpinski murmured, *"Thank you, God - with your help a thousand things are possible. I'm still in with a chance here, although it's all in the hands of the Russian Navy now."*

Whilst waiting for Gregorovitch to return from the Central Operations Room, Chelpinsky took a sip of his now tepid coffee, grimaced and thought, *"So, only 20 billion dollars has been mentioned. Where is the remainder of the money I wonder. I will have to speak to Mikhail Kotov myself about that, see if he knows anything."*

"Someone else has obviously been dipping their fingers in the till to the tune of 6 billion dollars. Who could that be, I wonder?"

The Russian Kontradmiral, Boris Slavonovitch, a hard-faced, hard drinking, long-serving and experienced realist, rather surprisingly hadn't questioned his orders, particularly after he'd read the copy of the letter of authority signed by the Comrade Supreme Commander himself. He couldn't, and wouldn't, argue with that.

An extremely astute man, he recognised the importance and urgency of the task, so Slavonovitch had immediately instructed his staff to check out which Russian naval vessels were in the Gulf of Finland area where the 'MV Chama Globtik' would be passing through, and also to ascertain if they had the capability to intercept and stop the ship dead in the water.

After some scrabbling around, it was established that the nearest vessel available for tasking in the area was the Russian Hunter/Killer submarine, (a Victor III Shchuka Class Nuclear Attack Sub) - 'The Kaluga' which was out at sea on a standard routine covert patrol, submerged and heading for the North Sea - its primary mission to disrupt, torment and test the British Royal Navy.

The Kontradmiral considered it a bit of overkill having to use a Hunter/Killer submarine for a routine 'Stop and Search' mission, but he'd had very little choice in the matter.

Time was of the essence and orders were orders, especially when those orders emanated from the Comrade Supreme Commander sat in his office at the epicentre of the scorpion's web - the Kremlin.

The Kontradmiral had been told precisely what the contents of the cargo container were, their importance to the President and that those contents had to be handled with extreme care whilst being transferred from the Iraqi ship to the submarine and thence on to Russia.

The Captain of the submarine, 'The Kaluga,' the doughty Captain 1st Class Grigory Avdiky Pentovitch, had received a flash signal directly from the Kontradmirals' Operations Room, giving him all of the background information and instructing him precisely what his new priority task was, i.e. to have the 'MV Chama Globtik,' located, stopped, boarded and then the contents of a large cargo container transferred to his sub.

The authority of the Comrade Supreme Commander was also alluded to in the message, just to add whatever juice was necessary.

Pentovitch knew that he wouldn't be able to transfer the large, ungainly cargo container itself onto his submarine and so would have to make arrangements for the cargo container to be located, opened and emptied of its contents, which were then to be cross-loaded over to his sub.

Not only that, he knew that he'd have to act swiftly getting the task completed because the Captain of the 'MV Chama Globtik' would undoubtedly radio for assistance. The job had to be done and dusted, then he had to be out of the area before anyone could come to rescue the ship.

Captain Pentovitch knew, for instance, that the Americans had a number of destroyers and guided missile frigates operating in the Baltic area and that they'd make every effort to come to the assistance of the stricken 'MV Chama Globtik,' particularly if they were aware that a Russian Hunter/Killer submarine was involved in an illegal act of piracy.

The Americans, he knew, relished a challenge, particularly when they were up against the Russian Navy.

Captain (1st Class) Pentovitch had had some unusual tasks allocated to him during his time in the submarine service and like every other Russian officer, his was not to reason why, but just to obey orders. After all, he wanted to be at least a Kontradmiral himself one day.

How strange, though, that he should be heaving to somewhere out in the middle of the Gulf of Finland, boarding a civilian ship and then transferring some 20 billion American dollars to his sub, oh - and apparently offering to give a passenger a lift home to Russia.

The Kontradmiral had also made it quite clear that if so much as a one dollar note went missing from the load then Pentovitch would be held personally responsible. The full amount of money was to be handed over to the Russian FSB representative who would be waiting with bated breath for his to return to Saint Petersburg, by the fastest and safest possible means.

Captain Pentovitch had also been tasked to ensure that the passenger, called Telenaz Hikmat, was also to be taken off the ship and brought back to Saint Petersburg. It was emphasised to Pentovitch that the man Hikmat was not to be treated as a prisoner but as an honoured guest and granted every courtesy. He didn't need to know anything else.

Hikmat, Captain Pentovitch was informed, was actually a Russian who held the rank of full Colonel and was to be treated accordingly.

The cargo ship's progress was being monitored by several Russian satellites and Pentovitch was given the precise co-ordinates to help him locate the 'MV Chama Globtik.' Once the sub had closed with the ship, he would then surface and get the task completed as quickly and efficiently as possible.

"*And here's me thinking that this was going to be just another boring patrol, tweaking the British lion's tail,*" thought Pentovitch, who in reality enjoyed a different challenge and was certain that one way or another, and despite the threat of horrendous repercussions, he might just be able to get his sticky mitts on a few of those dollars for himself.

"*Captain,*" said Pentovitch's Executive Officer, "*the ship is directly ahead of us and has stopped all her engines, as ordered.*" The Captain nodded and smiled, then ordered, "*Up periscope!*"

There was a quiet, silky swish as the submarine's periscope was raised. Pentovitch then clamped his eyes to the periscope's rubber eye-piece and examined the 'MV Chama Globtik' closely. Once the Captain was satisfied that the cargo ship was stationery and wallowing, he then swivelled the periscope around 360 degrees to check that there was no other shipping in the area that might pose a problem. Happily, it was all clear.

The submarine's radar had previously confirmed that there were no hostiles in the skies either, so they were good to go. *"All clear above! Stop engines! Blow all tanks and surface!"* he ordered. Pentovitch knew that he wouldn't have much time to board the 'MV Chama Globtik' and carry out his task.

He knew that the Captain of the 'MV Chama Globtik' would be attempting to send out a message that his ship was 'under attack' - despite being warned that he was forbidden to do so. Either that or someone on board the ship would try and summon assistance by simply making an emergency call using a 'cell-phone.

The Technical Officer on board 'The Kaluga' had ordered his staff to electronically 'jam' or scramble any of the radio messages that were being sent out from the ship, but Pentovitch was conscious that his main problem would be that of someone, somewhere, eyeballing them via satellite and monitoring the proceedings. There was also a chance that a passing aircraft might pick up an SOS and re-transmit it.

That 'someone' would more than likely be the infernal Americans or the interfering Brits. Pentovitch didn't have long to get the job done and was eager to get started.

The deadly looking Russian submarine, surfaced close to the port side of the stationery 'MV Chama Globtik' and even though the submarine itself was hugely impressive, it was dwarfed by the size of the cargo ship.

Up on the bridge of his submarine, Captain Pentovitch noted with satisfaction that the crew of the 'MV Chama Globtik' had, as instructed, opened a side-loading portal of the ship, just above its load-line, and were lowering a rigid gangway so that the armed Russians could clamber on board without too much difficulty.

Captain Pentovitch turned to his ever loyal Exec and said, *"I will board the ship myself, and speak to the Master."*

His Exec nodded, *"Very good Captain. And if anything should go wrong?"* *"That is highly unlikely, Evgeni, but if anything does go wrong I will let you know and then you are to send as many armed men as you can spare over to the ship as soon as possible."* ordered Pentovitch.

He continued, *"They are to open fire only if fired upon. We have to succeed with this mission and time is of the essence, for obvious reasons,"* said Pentovitch.

The Exec nodded again, *"I will have an enhanced boarding party fully armed and stood by, Captain. They can be sent across to the ship at a moment's notice."* "Excellent, now let us manoeuvre alongside the ship and get as close as we can," ordered Baranov.

Captain Pentovitch, accompanied by several armed sailors, clambered onto the vertical gangway, and boarded the 'MV Chama Globtik.' Fortunately the fully laden ship lay low in the relatively calm sea, so it wasn't too difficult getting on board.

Once on board the ship they were met by a nervous ship's officer who saluted Pentovitch and politely asked him and his party to accompany him to the bridge.

On arrival at the bridge, Pentovitch saluted the ship's Master and introduced himself, *"Captain, my respects, sir. I am Captain 1st Class Gregory Avdiky Baranov of the Russian Navy."*

The Captain of the 'MV Chama Globtik,' a small but very neat and precise Captain Kassim Ashabi, deliberately failed to return the Russian's salute and replied icily, *"And to what do I owe the 'honour' of being stopped and boarded in international waters? I am surprised, Captain, at this act of piracy! Russia and Iraq are supposed to be allies, are they not!"*

Captain Pentovitch nodded, *"Indeed they are, Captain. My deepest respects and my sincere apologies for having stopped and boarded your ship without permission. I mean you no insult. By way of explanation, I have been tasked by my government to remove the contents of a specific cargo container that you are shipping to Iraq. Once that is completed, I will be on my way and you may proceed on yours."*

Captain Ashabi asked, *"How kind of you. And what, may I ask, is so important about the contents of this obviously very special cargo container?"* Pentovitch smiled, *"With respect, you do not really need to know that, Captain, but let me assure you that once the job is completed I will be on my way and out of your hair."*

Captain Ashabi removed his hat and wiped his sweating brow with a crisp white handkerchief, revealing that he was as bald as a billiard ball, *"An unfortune turn of phrase, Captain!"* he said to the now slightly embarrassed Russian officer.

Captain Ashabi pointed at the deck of his ship where there were hundreds of containers lashed down. *"It doesn't take the brains of an Imam to see that there are very many cargo containers on board my ship. How do you expect me to locate yours at such short notice?"*

"Let us not play games with each other, Captain." replied Captain Pentovitch, *"I know for a fact that the cargo container I am seeking was the last one to be placed on board your ship before you set sail from the Port of Rotterdam."*

Captain Ashabi smiled and nodded, *"I must congratulate you, you are well informed, sir."*

Pentovitch smiled disarmingly, *"Yes, I am, - it goes with the job. Incidentally, Captain, you have a passenger on board, an Iraqi diplomat named Telenaz Hikmat."* Captain Ashabi replied, *"That is correct. He is my honoured guest." "Please send for him!"* ordered Captain Pentovitch.

A nonplussed looking Captain Ashabi turned and instructed one of his officers to go and fetch Telenaz Hikmat from his cabin.

On arrival on the bridge, Telenaz shook hands with Pentovitch and said, *"Captain, I am Telenaz Hikmat, or should I say, Colonel Mikhail Kotov."* Captain Pentovitch saluted him, *"Colonel, Captain (1st Class) Grigory Arkidy Pentovitch - at your service."*

"I am delighted to make your acquaintance, Colonel. Can I offer you a lift home?" said a smiling Pentovitch. *"How very kind of you, Captain. I am pleased and to be honest more than a little relieved to take you up on the offer,"* replied Colonel Kotov.

Colonel Kotov sighed, *"It will be so wonderful to see Mother Russia again, after all this time. There will have been many changes since I left there as a much younger man so many years ago."* Pentovitch replied, *"I think that you will be pleasantly surprised, Colonel."*

An intrigued Captain Ashabi was listening very carefully to the exchange between the two men, knowing that he would have to repeat their conversation, word for word, to the fearsome Iraqi Secret Service, the Mukhabarat, once he'd docked his ship in Khor al Zubair.

"*Right*," said Pentovitch, "*we just need to locate the relevant cargo container, 'break bulk' as they say and then transfer its contents over to my sub, then we can submerge and be on our way home.*"

"*I just might be able to help you there, Captain Pentovitch,*" said Colonel Kotov, "*you see, I arranged for an electronic locator to be placed inside the container, just before it was sealed - as a safety precaution you understand.*" Pentovitch smiled.

Kotov pulled out what looked like a small cell-phone from his pocket, "*This little gadget here will show us precisely where the all-important container is.*"

Pentovitch turned to Captain Ashabi and said, "*Captain, I would like your full co-operation with this aspect of the operation. Once my task is completed I will be out of your way and you can continue with your journey. If everyone does as they are told, then you have my word that no one on your ship will be harmed.*"

Captain Ashabi nodded, "*I will do what I must to assist you, and your men, Captain. However, I am duty bound to point out to you that you are committing an act of piracy on the high-seas and because of that I will be submitting a formal 'Captain's Protest' to my government at the earliest opportunity.*"

Pentovitch nodded, "*That, sir, is your prerogative. In the meantime, we had better make a start. My men will locate then open the cargo container and transfer its contents across to my submarine. I do not want any of your crew to touch anything or be involved in any way, other than perhaps a crane operator."*

"Let me assure you that anyone, including the crane operator, who disobeys my instructions will be shot and thrown overboard."

Captain Ashabi bristled, *"That is outrageous!"* he said, then sighed, *"Very well, I will instruct one of my officers to have a crane operator stood by and if I may, I would also like to make an announcement to the crew over the ship's tannoy so that they are aware of what's happening,"* he said. Pentovitch nodded, and said, *"You may proceed, Captain, but please be quick about it."*

Some two hours later, once the relevant container had been located and the cross-loading task completed, after bidding farewell to a disgruntled Captain Ashabi and thanking him for his co-operation, Captain Pentovitch, Colonel Mikhail Kotov and all of the American dollars had been transferred safely over to the Russian submarine.

Once everything and everyone was safely secured on board the sub, it's hatches were battened down and it was made ready to submerge.

As 'The Kaluga' sank beneath the waves, a relieved Captain Pentovitch was informed by his Exec that an American warship had been detected steaming its way to the area at a high rate of knots, obviously to investigate what was happening to the 'MV Chama Globtik.'

Unfortunately for the Americans they would be far too late arriving to prevent the Russian's departure. Even now the 'The Kaluga' was running deep and heading quietly for Saint Petersburg.

Captain Pentovitch handed over temporary control of the sub to his Exec and went to have a closer look at the cargo. When he saw just how many of the plastic-wrapped bundles of American dollars there were, guarded closely by armed sailors, he just sighed and thought to himself *"Just one teensy-weensy bundle. If only!"*

Ж

CHAPTER FIFTEEN

'TO THE RESCUE!'

"Why so gloomy, my little Scottish amigo? You look as if you've lost a rouble and found a kopek!" a solicitous Graham asked Mike. *"No, it's much worse than that, my friend. Ed De Jong's just been on the 'phone,"* said Mike.

"From the look on your face, he was obviously the bearer of grim tidings. What's the matter then, the price of gold dropped has it?" joked Graham. Mike sighed and shook his head, *"No, it's more serious than that, pal!"*

"What's up then?" asked Graham

"Ed rang to tell me that our wee mate Kassim Bashara was arrested by the Russian FSB at his compound in Saint Petersburg yesterday and that they've flown him to Moscow!" said Mike. *"Oh no, that's bloody awful news! How the hell did they latch onto him?"* asked Graham.

Mike sighed, *"Apparently one of Kassim's swivel-eyed employee 'turned Queen's evidence' and told the Russians all about Kassim's involvement with the theft of the dollars from the Sheremetyevo compound."*

"Oh my God, that's shocking news," said a now gloomy Graham. *"The bloke that coughed to the FSB was dealt with swiftly, but that doesn't help poor old Kassim,"* said Mike.

"To make matters infinitely worse," Mike continued, *"the Russian Security Services have somehow or other managed to get their sticky mitts on the 20 billion dollars that were being shipped back to Iraq, so things, technically speaking, have gone completely tits-up!"*

"Does that mean that they're onto us three, four if you include Rosti, as well?" asked Graham. *"Don't think so, not yet anyway, but it'll only be a matter of time before they beat the information out of Kassim. You know what those FSB bastards are like once they get the bit between their teeth*," said Mike, shaking his head sorrowfully.

"So what's gone on then?" asked Graham *"Well,"* said Mike, *"it appears that our friend Kassim was hauled in and given a severe seeing to by the Saint Petersburg branch of the FSB, and was then choppered off to Moscow. According to Ed, Kassim's currently residing in the cellars of the Lubyanka Prison - and we know what'll be happening to him down there."*

"Hell fire, that is shocking news. How did Ed find out about it?" asked Graham. *"He got a call from his mate Boris 'The Scorpion' Krensky,"* telling him that General Chelpinski and his henchman Colonel Gregorovitch were *at the root of all this and that they'd been tasked to sort*

the robbery out by no less a man than the Russian President, Boris Baronovski himself," replied Mike.

"I might have guessed it. That bloody horrible man General Igor Chelpinski, and his mate Colonel Ivanski Gregorypeckski. Turned up like two bad pennies again. You know, Mike, Chelpinsky still hasn't forgiven us for the time when we left him and his henchman to rot in the 'Hidden Library at the Lubyanka Prison!" said Graham.

"Aye," said Mike, *"that's undoubtedly why Chelps and Ivanski have taken a personal interest. Bit of revenge."*

"So what does Ed intend that we do about it?" asked Graham.

"Well, as Ed said, we can't just leave Kassim rotting in the Lubyanka Prison, so it looks like we'll have to mount a rescue operation and get him out of there," said Mike.

"Ed says that as far as he knows Kassim hasn't told them of our involvement, as yet, but it's obviously just a matter of time before he coughs. You can well imagine what will happen then." said Mike. Graham nodded, *"Yes, then the bastards will be coming after us."*

Mike nodded and said, *"Aye, Chelps will be sending his FSB lads over here to try and discover what we've done with the rest of the money. Anyway, Ed's on his way over here from Amsterdam, and he'll be arriving at Humberside Travelport later this afternoon. He wants us* to get our heads together and try to come up with some sort of rescue plan for Kassim."

Mike looked at his watch, "*We're going to have to get a move on with this. Every second counts.*" "*It's going to be bloody difficult isn't it,*" said Graham, "*particularly as you're still down to the one 'T3-Travellator.*"

Mike nodded, "*Aye, the replacement 'T3' won't be ready for a couple more weeks and the other 'T-3' is in the workshop for servicing and repair.*" "*Repair?*" asked Graham.

"*Aye,*" said Mike, "*it's just returned from a journey to the Battle of Hastings in 1066. It had hundreds of arrows stuck all over the outer casing would you believe! Bloody archers!*"

"*It's that Duke of Normandy! I never liked him; he was a nasty piece of work. Typical frog, ugly bastard as well!*" said Graham.

Ed nodded in agreement then continued, "*I'm assured by our Technical Manager, Jason King, that the 'T3' should be up and running by tomorrow morning at the latest. Thank goodness we've got Jase working for us. Top man!*"

Graham said, "*I was just thinking, Mike. Why do we have to go to the Lubyanka Prison to rescue Kassim? Why can't we just 'Time-Travel' over to Kassim's place in Saint Petersburg and arrive there prior to his arrest, then we can just whiz him away before the Russian bad boys arrive on the scene?"*

Mike nodded, *"Yeah, that's one solution I suppose. I hadn't considered that. Let's see what Ed thinks about it when he gets here. In the meantime, I'll go and put the kettle on. A nice brew of calming Yorkshire tea wouldnae go amiss."*

A few hours later a concerned looking Ed arrived. *"Hi guys, great to see you."* he said. *"Hi Ed, and it's nice to see you again,"* replied Mike, shaking hands with him. *"I just wish that the circumstances could have been a little bit better,"* said Ed.

"Aye, it was terrible news about Kassim," said Mike, *"Come on, sit down and take the weight off your clogs my friend, then we can discuss what we're going to do to get this sorted. Graham's come up with a wee suggestion that you might think is worthy of consideration."*

Ed sat down, *"I don't suppose there's a chance of a decent cup of char before we get cracking?"* he asked. *"Kettle's just boiled,"* said Mike, *"unless you'd like something a bit stronger?" "No, tea's just fine, thanks,"* said Ed.

A couple of hours later the lads had decided that the best course of action they could take was to jump into the 'T3-Travellator' and fly back in time to Saint Petersburg to warn Kassim that he was about to be arrested, then move him and his immediate family to safety in Amsterdam.

Ed would then get the Kassim family's relocation sorted out and they could take things from there.

Kassim's immediate family would have to be removed from Russian soil to avoid any further repercussions from the FSB, who would undoubtedly move hell and earth trying to find them.

Ed said, *"Well, as we're going to travel back in time, logically I don't suppose that there's any immediate rush is there?"*

Mike shook his head and said, *"Well, you say that Ed, but at this precise moment things will probably be very uncomfortable for Kassim down there in the Lubyanka cells. God alone knows what he'll be going through."*

"Yes, but surely we could save him from all that by getting him before he's arrested, couldn't we?" asked Graham.

"That's right, Graham, but speaking in the here and now, he'll be under the lash and suffering," said Mike.

Graham shook his head, *"It's bloody complex is this 'Time-Travel' lark!"* he said, *"I mean if we get to Kassim before the FSB does, then his arrest won't have taken place, but in actuality as they've got him now then he'll be being mistreated as we speak. I need a drink to help me clear my head."*

"You know what, you're right Mike," said Ed, *"and on second thoughts, I'd prefer to go straight to the Lubyanka,*

rescue Kassim then time-transfer over to Saint Petersburg to pick up Kassim's close family before legging it back to Amsterdam."

"I have several contacts in Turkey and can arrange for Kassim, his wife and kids to be tucked away there for the rest of their lives, in complete anonymity. The rest of his cousins and so forth can just disappear into the woodwork for a while. We can make sure that they'll all be looked after financially."

"Sounds like a good plan to me," said Mike.

Graham tutted, *"You know, ;ads, I'm never going to get my head around this 'Time-Travel' business. I mean, if we went back in time to get him before all this Lubyanka business happened - then what's happening to him now wouldn't be, would it?"*

"Don't over-think it, mate," said Mike, *"just go with the flow."*

"But won't we be interfering with the natural scheme of things with all of this?" asked Graham. Mike nodded, *"Yes, we will, but needs must when the devil drives - the devil in this case being the Russian FSB. Anyway, we can't, in all conscience, leave our mate Kassim in their hands, not when we have the ability to do something about it."*

"Suppose you're right, Mike. We've had first-hand experience of that git Chelpinsky and seen what he and

Gregorovitch can do to the prisoners in those cells, and it isn't very pretty," replied Graham.

"The only problem that I can foresee," said Mike, *"is that currently we're down to the one 'T3-Travellator' and if our Technical Manager, Jason King, can't get that up and running a bit sharpish, then we're well and truly snookered."*

Mike stood up, *"Come on lads, let's go over to the workshop and see how the repairs to the 'T3' are coming along. He's a superb technician is Jase, ex-RAF you know. He'll be pulling out all the stops - and all of those bloody arrows, in order to get it operational and back into service."*

Ж

CHAPTER SIXTEEN

'TIME TO GO HOME'

Utterly exhausted and trembling uncontrollably, as if suffering from some terrible ague, a grey-faced 'Prisoner Kassim Bashara' was perched uncomfortably on the edge of an unforgiving cold metal chair. The immovable chair was bolted to the bare, rough concrete floor of his current no-star accommodation, in the cellars of Moscow's infamous Lubyanka Prison. Neither the chair or Kassim were destined to be going anywhere in the foreseeable future.

Every muscle in Kassim's bruised and battered body ached from the beatings he'd received and, because he had been denied anything to drink since he'd been arrested, Kassim was so dehydrated that he was literally dying of thirst. Food was just a fond memory.

Since he'd been incarcerated in the Lubyanka Prison he'd been slapped and beaten, bright lights had constantly been shone in his face and he hadn't been permitted to sleep. Sleep deprivation was just another implement in the tool box of tortures used with impunity by the FSB. For inmates, the Lubyanka Prison was hell on earth.

Despite all that, Kassim had bravely and resolutely refused to tell the FSB what they so desperately wanted to know. He and they knew that he wouldn't be able to hold out for very much longer.

The unfortunate Kassim was strapped tightly to the legs of the chair with sharp edged nylon ties, ankles red raw and bleeding, his arms fully stretched out in front of him and handcuffed hands secured to a chunky metal ring embedded in the centre of the table, all ensuring that Kassim was completely defenceless and vulnerable. He was unable to protect himself from a seemingly endless series of kicks, slaps and blows, each one coming from an unexpected direction.

As both the table and chair were firmly anchored to the floor of the cell they were immovable and couldn't be picked up to use as weapons by victims, not that Kassim had any strength left to put up a fight. Frighteningly, the centre of the chair seat had been removed so that it resembled an open lavatory seat. Kassim dreaded to think what that might be used for, but had a fair idea.

It was a hopeless situation, from which the only escape was either blessed unconsciousness or death.

It had been Kassim's third interrogation of the day. He and his tormentors knew full well that he wouldn't be able to hold out for very much longer. Much as he didn't want to, eventually he'd crumble and tell them everything that they wanted to know.

His once handsome face was swollen and very badly bruised and he looked like he'd done several rounds with Mike Tyson. His front teeth had been loosened, and he was having difficulty breathing because his nostrils were blocked with dried blood from where Chelpinski and Gregorovitch had cruelly and relentlessly back-handed, kicked and punched him. They fired seemingly endless questions at him, each question followed by a vicious blow.

Kassim's eyes were red with fatigue, his left eye badly swollen and closed. He could barely see, so there was no way that he could try and avoid any of the incoming blows, he just had to sit there, absorbing the cruel and unjust punishment.

Lounging comfortably on a chair at the other side of the table, directly in front of Kassim, the sneering General Chelpinsky, enjoying every second of the naked brutality, had deliberately 'let it slip' that most of the stolen American dollars had been recovered and that he was determined to find out what had happened to the remainder. Chelpinski also wanted to know the names of the others involved in the robbery, so that they could be brought down to the Lubyanka cells and invited to reveal the whereabouts of the remainder of the stolen money, with varying degrees of encouragement. The prospect of doling out further beatings excited the General.

Chelpinsky had assured Kassim that he wouldn't be given a moment's peace until he'd coughed up the information. Once he'd told Chelpinski what he wanted to know, he been assured that not only would he be given food and water, but the beatings would stop immediately and he would be allowed to get some sleep. A desperate Kassim knew that to be an out and out lie. Once he'd told them everything they wanted to know, he'd no longer be of any use to Chelpinski and his friends and would be disposed of.

Kassim, of course, knew most of the details and whereabouts of those that had been involved in the robbery, after all he'd been a key member of the team, but he genuinely didn't know what had happened to the rest of the money once it had left Saint Petersburg on board the 'MV Solar Star.' That information hadn't been imparted to him by Ed, nor was he particularly interested.

To ensure the team's safety, and as a matter of principle, Ed intentionally kept every aspect of the robbery compartmentalised and had deliberately not told Kassim about anything other than his own involvement. Key elements of information had deliberately been kept on a 'Need to Know' basis.

As he didn't need to know what was happening to the money once it had left Saint Petersburg, Kassim hadn't been told about it - and quite honestly couldn't have cared less. He'd been paid up front very handsomely and was as happy as a sand-boy with that.

Kassim was well aware that he couldn't tell Chelpinsky what he so desperately wanted to know and that the brutal and psychopathic General didn't believe his consistent denials. If anything, things were destined to get worse for Kassim. He was in a hopeless situation and could see no way out of it.

This was, Kassim thought, much like the days when so-called witches were interrogated by the Spanish Inquisition. 'Trial by Ordeal,' where the accused was strapped to a ducking stool and lowered into water, such as a river or a pond. If the accused didn't sink and floated on the surface, he or she was deemed to be guilty and taken away to be hanged. If they sank to the bottom of the water and drowned, they were deemed to be innocent! "*It must have been a politician that thought that one up*," thought a battered Kassim. He was now in a very similar 'no-win' situation.

He fleetingly thought that Chelpinski's title should be changed from 'Leader of Soviet Security and Intelligence Services' to that of 'Witchfinder General.' Chelpinski was a heartless bastard who obviously loved his work, particularly if there was a spot of torturing to be had.

The cell door suddenly swung open and the General's smirking henchman, the ever enthusiastic Colonel Ivanski Gregorovitch, wheeled a sturdy two tiered metal trolley into the cell, looking for all the world like a cheerful hotel waiter delivering dinner.

Peering through his one good eye, Kassim could just about make out the top shelf of the trolley, on which, neatly laid out, was a selection of mortifying surgical instruments, the purpose of which at Kassim didn't even dare think about. On the second shelf of the trolley sat two hefty car batteries and a set of jump leads.

A frightened Kassim tried his hardest to swallow, but couldn't. This was, he thought, like something out of one of his worst nightmares.

"Feast your good eye on this little lot my friend," said Gregorovitch, waving his hand towards the instruments, *"I borrowed these surgical instruments from the local Mortuary, they'd finished with them for today. Wasn't that kind of them. They're a bit sticky, but they'll have to do."*

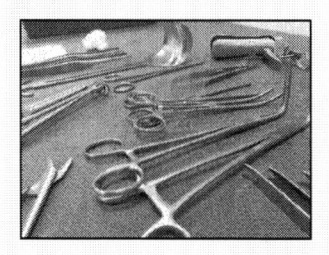

Kassim's heart sank as he watched Gregorovitch pull on a pair of heavy industrial rubber gloves.

Gregorovitch then picked up a pair of sharp surgical scissors from the tray, walked across to Kassim's chair, hunkered down and reached underneath the 'lavatory' seat before carefully removing the gusset of Kassim's soiled trousers, exposing his genitals. *"Aha, the family jewels are revealed,"* said a cheerful Gregorovitch, *"we're just about ready to begin."* *"I can tell you nothing!"* screamed Kassim, receiving a slap across the face from Gregorovitch for his troubles.

The watching General Chelpinsky knew that he himself wasn't quite out of the woods with the Russian President yet. Chelpinsky had claimed most of the glory for recovering the $20 billion, but President Baronovski had continued to insist that he find out where the remainder of the stolen money was and wanted to know why it hadn't been recovered within the time-frame that Chelpinski had been given.

Fortunately for him, the General had been granted just a few more days to get to the bottom of things, although it was made clear to him that a further extension would not be granted and that he would be made to suffer the dire consequences in the event of failure.

Chelpinski had experienced another very icy, mercifully short, interview with President Baronovski at which, much to Chelpinsky's surprise, the aged ex-President Saddam Hussein had also been present, sat in his wheelchair, glaring at him throughout with evil and rheumy eyes, a foul-smelling cheroot clamped firmly between his teeth.

The 'dynamic-duo' of Presidents glaring at him had made even the veteran torturer General 'Chiller' Chelpinsky tremble with fear. The two Presidents were the very epitome of evil. Chelpinsky knew that he wouldn't be given any more chances. The many graveyards in and around Moscow were full of indispensable people.

Chelpinski suddenly reached out across the table and with the outstretched palm of his hand gave Kassim Bashara another fierce slap across the side of his head, expertly cupping his hand so that the force of the blow caused the poor unsuspecting man's ear-drum to perforate. Kassim screamed in agony.

Wiping his hand on his trouser leg, Chelpinski snarled, *"I am warning you for the very last time, Kassim Bashara, my patience has run out. Tell me what I want to know, or I will hand this interrogation over to Colonel Gregorovitch here who I can assure you will not be half as gentle and considerate as I have been!"* Before Kassim could reply, Chelpinsky slapped Kassim again, this time on his other ear.

A thoroughly dazed Kassim's head dropped forward, all of his strength sapped, but bravely he remained defiantly silent.

An enraged Chelpinsky, seeing that he was getting nowhere, leapt to his feet, sending his chair skittering across the cell, *"Very well, you had your chance,"* he hissed. He turned to Colonel Gregorovitch, *"Looks like it's over to you, Ivanski."*

"Why, thank you, General. I'll see what I can do," said a smiling Ivanski as he wheeled the metal trolley and its contents over to the table. Reaching down, he connected one end of the jump leads to a battery, using the positive and negative crocodile clips, then theatrically tapped the opposite ends of the leads together so that they arced and sparked.

"Shall I have a quick dabble with his private parts, or should I just go straight for the nipples, Comrade General?" The General shook his head, *"I don't care what you do to him, Ivanski, just so long as his tongue remains relatively intact, well, for the moment anyway,"* he said.

Once again Gregorovitch tapped the ends of the jump leads together and grinned as they sparked, *"You know what, I think I'll connect these crocodile clips to the metal seat of the chair, just to give you an idea of what to expect,"* he said to Kassim.

Kassim nearly fainted with fear. He had prided himself on being a tough, resilient man but the threat of what was about to happen to him was just too much to contemplate.

He had done his best not to reveal the names of his friends but his resolve was weakening by the second. Apart from anything else, Kassim couldn't tell them what they wanted to know because he didn't know anything other than the bare bones of the robbery, but his tormentors wouldn't believe him.

Suddenly dropping the battery leads down onto the floor, Ivanski turned and picked up a pair of substantial and shiny metal surgical pincers, clicked them a couple of times to ramp up the drama then said to Kassim, *"Wait a moment, let's do this differently, shall we. The batteries will keep for the moment!"*

Holding the pincers in front of Kassim's face, he said, *"These pincers, my friend, are my personal favourites. They were designed for the efficient surgical removal of various digits and soft tissue, normally in a hospital type scenario and so obviously with the need for anaesthetic."* Smiling, he continued, *"Unfortunately, Kassim, today when I use these on you, you will not have the benefit of pain relief, but that's all part of the fun of it."*

Kassim gave an involuntary shudder.

Wiggling one of Kassim's fingers, Gregorovitch said, *"We'll make a start with your fingers. The pincers are, as you would expect, made from the finest extremely sharp surgical steel, designed so that the 'patient' - you - will feel very little pain as each digit is removed, well not at first anyway. Don't be disappointed though, let me assure you that the pain comes shortly afterwards, in spades."*

"Now, Kassim, you have no doubt noticed that I can that attach these pincers to a length of copper wiring which I clip to those other leads that you see hanging off the trolley, they in turn are attached to the battery terminals, a good word that - terminal."

"Once linked together they produce a delightful 'double whammy,' the electricity that they generate heats the pincers and also produces an electrical power surge that quite amusingly makes the recipients go rigid and their hair stand on end. Fortunately I have this excellent pair of well insulated gloves to protect me."

"Unfortunately, Kassim, as you now have a prison haircut and your head has been shaven, we won't be seeing that particular effect today. Still, can't have everything, can we."
Gregorovitch tantalisingly clicked the pincers together, *"So, we are just about good to go. With your permission, General?"* Chelpinski smiled and nodded, *"Crack on, Ivanski!"*

Ivanski turned and snapped the jump-lead clips onto the wire hanging from the pincer handles. *"Just give me a moment or two to let the current flow and for the pliers to heat up, then we can begin."*

"Fortunately the grips of the pincers are also well insulated, so it won't be too uncomfortable for me, although I can't promise the same for you."

"Now, what happens next, Kassim, is that once I remove, say, your thumb, then the blades of the electronically heated pliers automatically seal the open wound, ostensibly so that you don't lose too much blood. Clever that, isn't it. Naturally it will sting a little, but then that's all down to you - you can make all of this stop at any time."

"You'll get twenty one opportunities to speak out and then I will start on other areas of what remains of your pathetic body. In case you were wondering, that's ten fingers, ten toes and a certain other appendage. "

After about a minute or so, Ivanski examined the now glowing pincers and said, *"Ah, that should just about do it."* He placed the pincers on the table and pulled a packet of cigarettes out of his top pocket, extracted a cigarette then lit it on one of the blades of the now red-hot pincers. The cigarette lighting routine was a 'party trick' he often used to further intimidate his intended victims and one he greatly enjoyed doing, using it to drag things out. Sometimes he smoked the whole cigarette before starting to torture his victims, flicking the hot ash on their bare skin.

On several previous occasions his prisoners had confessed long before the pincers were applied to their bodies, but Gregorovitch always removed a couple of their digits anyway, usually starting with the little finger, just to prove that he meant business and to encourage the flow of information to continue.

Taking a puff of his glowing cigarette, he knelt down in front of the bare-footed Kassim, and examined his toes closely. Ivanski tutted, *"Mmm, slight touch of athletes foot there my friend. You'll have to keep an eye on that."* Without any warning he stubbed the cigarette out on Kassim's big toe. A rigid Kassim very nearly fainted with the agonising pain.

Gregorovitch sniggered and said, *"It says on the packet that smoking's bad for you!"* then stood up and reached across the table, grabbing Kassim's hand and wiggling his little finger. *"This little piggy went to market, this little piggy stayed at home - and this little piggy, that's you Kassim - well, you're going to squeal all the way home!"*

He picked up the glowing pincers and slowly moved them towards Kassim's little finger, whilst Kassim looked helplessly on.

Meanwhile, General Chelpinsky lounged back in his chair, smirking and enjoying the 'entertainment' which he considered as being just one of the perks of his job. He'd give Gregorovitch a few more minutes to have some fun before taking over from him.

Suddenly, and without any warning, there was a loud whooshing sound from behind General Chelpinsky. Both Chelpinsky and Gregorovitch turned swiftly and saw, to their immense surprise, that a 'T3-Travellator' had dematerialised in a corner of the cell.

Chelpinski leapt to his feet and said, *"What the f......"* He paused as the door on the 'T3' slid open and a fierce looking Ed stepped out. Ed was holding a pistol which was pointed straight at the General's forehead.

Ed called out to Chelpinsky and Gregorovitch, *"Ah, still up to your nasty old party tricks, eh, gentlemen!"*

An astounded Kassim looked up at Ed and his jaw dropped. *"Ed, I don't believe it! I must be dreaming!"* he mumbled. *"Morning Kassim, me and the lads have come to rescue you from this hell on earth!"* said a smiling Ed. *"Allah be praised,"* said Kassim.

Mike and Graham stepped out of the 'T3-Travellator,' "*Morning Kassim, nice to see you!*" they said in unison. Mike turned towards Chelpinski and Gregorovitch and said, "*Morning chaps. Just in case you'd forgotten, him – Ed De Jong, me Mike Fraser and him Graham St Anier. Long-time no see!*"

Hand slyly reaching for his pistol, a sneering Chelpinski replied, "*Of course! I should have known all along that it would be you three - the three 'Time-Travel' stooges! Come to rescue another of your criminal friend's, have you?*"

Ed replied, "*Got it in one, Comrade - and I shouldn't touch your pistol if I were you. It would give me great pleasure to blast your balls off one at a time!*" "*That's if he's got a pair,*" said Mike. "*Now, both of you, get your hands in the air where we can see them!*" Ed ordered. Chelpinsky and Gregorovitch raised their hands.

Kassim was looking at Ed with an air of incredulity, firmly believing that he was hallucinating and in no doubt that the torture would begin again at any second.

Chelpinski muttered, "*It all makes sense now, Ivanski. The easy way in which the thieves gained access to the Security Compound at Sheremetyevo Airport, the burnt out wreckage in the corner of the hangar - it was a 'Time-Machine,' that alone should have set alarm bells ringing.*"

"Aye, you should have been a wee bit quicker on the uptake, Chelps, but then you and your oppo, old Gregory Peckski here, are not the brightest two stars in the Russian military firmament, are you!" said Mike cheerfully.

Turning to Chelpinski, Gregorovitch said, *"But General, we weren't really certain about that pile of smouldering ruins in the hangar, after all, there was very little of it left."* Still looking puzzled, Gregorovitch asked, *"Just who are these people, General, they look and sound vaguely familiar?"*

"Hell fire, he's as dim as a Toc H lamp is this lad!" said Graham. *"Aye, old Peckski is as thick as pig-shit if you ask me. Obviously some village in Russia is missing its idiot, eh Chelps?"* said Mike.

"Cast your mind back to the early 1960s, Ivanski, and the 'Hidden Library,'" said Chelpinski. Gregorovitch still looked blank. *"You'd better give him another clue, Chelps, he's not on receive yet,"* said Mike.

"Think Ivanski!" said Chelpinsky, *"These three criminals came to rescue the traitor and spy, Lieutenant Colonel Penkovsky!"* (*)

(*) - See 'Tinkering With Time.'

A light suddenly came on in the back of Ivanski's thick skull as realisation slowly dawned, *"Yes, of course! The 'Time-Travellers!"* A grinning Graham said, *"Ah, at last, the kopek drops! You know what lads, he's about as much use as a vegan in a tripe shop!"*

Turning to Mike, who was stood at his side, Ed said, *"Get their weapons Mike, before they try anything heroic."* Mike nodded and went over to the two Russian officers, removed their pistols, unloaded them, and threw the weapons into the 'T3.'

Mike winked at Chelpinski, nipped his cheek and said, *"Hello there Chelps, remember me, your old 'Jock' friend, Mike Fraser?"* Chelpinski sneered, *"Yes, I remember you now, Scotlander!"* Mike smiled and replied, *"Well, it's lovely tae bump into you again after all these years - and haven't you two done well for your wee selves. One a General and one a Colonel, no less. Whoever would have guessed it!"*

Chelpinski glared at Mike, his face a mask of undisguised hatred. *"Bastard!"* he said. Mike smiled, *"There's no need to be nice!"*

"By the way, Chelps," said a totally unphased Mike, his nose wrinkling, *"I notice that your mate Ivanski still hasn't done anything about his body odour problem. He's still a bit of a wee Russian stinker, eh!"*

Flushing bright red, Ivanski said, *"You are very brave, my friend, particularly when you have a loaded weapon in your hand."*

Mike stepped forward and without any warning hit Ivanski on the chin with a large, hairy, bunched Scottish fist. Ivanski's head snapped backwards and he fell down onto the cell floor like a large sack of spuds. *"I dinnae need a loaded weapon tae sort a wee shite like you oot, Peckski!"* said Mike.

Helping a dazed Gregorovitch back up onto to his feet, Chelpinski said, *"Do not let him provoke you, Ivanski. He is just taking advantage of the situation."* "Hey, Generalski," said Mike, *" you want tae be careful that you dinnae get a bunch of fives yourself, so I'd advise ye to shut your Russian cake-hole!"*

"Graham," said Ed, *"can you go and release our friend Kassim please."* Graham nipped across to Kassim, glanced at the handcuffs that secured him to the table then turned to a barely sensible Ivanski and snapped, *"Oy, dogs breath, the keys to the cuffs, now! Come on, snap it up, you bloody useless toe-rag, we haven't got all day!"*

A still dazed Ivanski reached into his trouser pocket and pulled out a handcuff key that he begrudgingly handed to Graham. Graham unlocked Kassim from the handcuffs, then used the pair of surgical pliers to snip through the plasticuffs holding his ankles before helping him to stand up. Kassim swayed and nearly collapsed. *"Steady, Kassim. Let me give you a hand,"* said Graham

"I can't begin to tell you just how good it is to see you, my friends," said a tearful Kassim, rubbing his chafed wrists, *"I have told these two swines nothing that they*

didn't already know." "What happened to your foot, Kassim, it's bleeding?" Mike asked him.

Pointing a wavering finger at Ivanski, Kassim said, *"That bastard stubbed a lit cigarette out on it." "That was very naughty, Peckski,"* said Mike, then chinned him again. Gregorovitch lurched backwards but this time managed to stay on his feet.

Nodding towards the two Russians, Ed said to Mike, *"Mike, use the handcuffs to secure those two bandits to the table will you. A wrist each." "My pleasure,"* replied Mike.

Mike waved Chelpinski and Gregorovitch over to the table, *"Come along ladies, shift your slack Russian arses!"* and then handcuffed them both to the solid metal ring that was firmly embedded into the surface of the table, using a single handcuff each. Stepping back and looking at them, Mike said, *"Och, you make such a pretty wee pair, joined at the wrists like that."*

"Better search their pockets Mike, Just check that they haven't got any more handcuff keys or weapons tucked away in there." said Ed.

Mike nodded then searched the two officers thoroughly, patting them down and even turning down the tops of their socks to see that there was nothing hidden away. *"All clear,"* he said cheerfully, *"although I have to say that the Colonels' socks are definitely a tad ripe!"*

"Right," said Ed, *"we'd better get Kassim on board our fiery chariot and head for home, gentlemen." "And what about us two?"* asked Chelpinsky, *"I suppose that you are going to execute us before you leave?"*

"Nothing would give me more pleasure than to give you two the 'Coup de Grâce,'" said Ed, *"but that's not the way we behave where we come from, General. We leave that sort of thing to scum-bags like you two."*

"In which case," sneered Chelpinski, *"you should warn you that once we are released, be in no doubt that we'll be coming after you!" "Jings!"* said Mike, *"guess what Chelps, we're crapping ourselves - not!"*

Shaking his head, Mike continued, *"And bad news, pal, I'm afraid that you won't be coming after us. You see, one of the benefits of having access to a 'Time-Machine' is that we are able to have a look at what's happened not only in the past but also take a peek at what happens in the future."*

"And your point is, Scotlander?" sneered Chelpinski.

"I shouldn't really be telling you this, but we've seen what's going tae happen to the pair of you - and let me assure you that it isn't going to be very pretty," replied Mike.

Chelpinsky spluttered, *"What do you mean?" "Well, let's put it this way, Chelps, I shouldnae start reading 'War and Peace' if I were you 'cos you're not going tae finish it!"* replied Mike.

"In fact," said Graham, *"you lads had better get used to these plush prison surroundings." "And of course those surgical instruments,"* said Mike, pointing at the wheeled trolley, *"because you're going to become very familiar with them both - only this time it'll be you on the receiving end!"* Colonel Gregorovitch had turned very pale by this time. *"Ignore them, Ivanski,"* said Chelpinski, *"they're talking nonsense."*

"Oh Mike," said Ed, tutting, *"you've spoilt the surprise now. By the way, General, did I mention that your Russian President, Comrade Baronovski, is on his way here as we speak?"*

Chelpinsky's eyes widened but other than that he failed to respond. *"Well, he is, so I suppose we'd better make a move,"* said Ed.

Elbowing Chelpinski in the ribs, causing him to gasp, a smiling Mike said, *"Hey, rather you than me, my friend. He'll have you reduced to the rank of Corporal before you know it, Chelps!"*

Ed looked down at his watch, *"President Baronovski will be arriving here in about ten minutes and when finds you two handcuffed to the table - and sees that your prisoner, our friend Kassim here, has escaped, he will be more than shall we say a little vexed."*

"Listen, all this unfortunate business here, we were just doing our duty you know," said Chelpinski, *"Can't we do some sort of deal?"* asked the suddenly desperate General. *"What do you mean, a deal?"* asked Ed.

"What would it take for you to release us from these handcuffs and let us accompany you in your 'Time-Machine,'" asked Chelpinski.

Ed shook his head, *"You and I both know that that's not going to happen, General. No, I'm afraid that you're just going to have to stay here and face the presidential ire!"*

Mike tutted, *"Och, I can just see it all now. The old Russkie 'Pressie' will be thrilled tae bits at what's gone on. Imagine Baronovski's face as you try to explain everything to him - it'll no be a pretty sight. I'm almost tempted to stay here and watch the fun and games. I wonder how you'll try and talk your way out of this one, eh, Chelpie my boy!"*

Glancing at his wristwatch, Graham said, *"I think that it's time we made tracks, lads, come on!"* Ed, Graham and Mike all helped the frail Kassim walk across to the 'T3' and then lifted him on board. Gently lowering him into one of the seats, Graham handed him a bottle of ice-cold water. *"Drink that slowly, Kassim,"* advised Graham. Kassim nodded and took a few sips from the bottle, *"Tastes better than the finest champagne,"* he said.

Turning to Chelpinski and Gregorovitch, Graham called out, *"TTFN then chaps; been nice bumping into you both again. Take care of yourselves and try to stay out of trouble. By the way, if you're ever passing through Beverley, do pop into the 'Dog and Duck' and join us for a pint."* "*Aye, do come and say hello,*" said Mike, both him and Graham chortling as Ed tapped the various console switches and the door of the 'T3-Travellator' started to close and seal them in.

A few seconds after the door had completely closed, the 'T3' began the complex materialisation process and set off on its journey through the ether - leaving the Lubyanka Prison just as quietly as it had arrived.

Chelpinski and Gregorovitch gazed helplessly at the empty space where the 'T-3' had been.

As they both sat there in the silence of the cell, sharing the chair and handcuffed to the table, Gregorovitch turned to Chelpinski and asked, "*So, where do we go from here, Comrade General?*" "*Well, I don't know about you, but I know precisely what I'm going to do, Ivanski,*" replied the General.

There was the sound of a slight crunch as Chelpinski bit down on the glass ampule of cyanide potassium that he'd had hidden inside his tooth for many years. "*The poison won't take too long to act,*" he said then flopped down onto the floor, gasping for breath, hanging from the table by his arm, a faint odour of almonds coming from his mouth.

"But General," said a panicking Gregorovitch, *"there was no need for you to do that! I know where there is a spare key for these handcuffs! There was still time for us to escape from here ..."*

Chelpinski, who had by that time turned blue as the poison he had swallowed kicked in, raised his head and gasped, *"Time for you maybe, but not for me. Escape from here whilst you can, Ivanski. Been nice knowing you."*

Chelpinski gave one final gasp, then his eyes rolled up into the back of his head and he slumped back onto the floor.

Gregorovitch was frozen to the spot. He certainly hadn't envisaged that happening, nor had he had the foresight to have an ampule of poison secreted about his person for use if needed. He couldn't have anything hidden in any of his teeth anyway, it would have been difficult as they were all solid metal.

After a few seconds gathering his senses, Ivanski scrabbled around under the table searching for the spare key that he knew was taped there for use in an emergency. He located the key then used it to release himself from the handcuffs.

Looking down at the body of Chelpinsky he thought, *"Well, that's one prediction that those damned 'Time-Travellers got right! Now, if I get a move on I've got just enough time to get out of here before that bastard Baronovski arrives and all hell breaks loose."*

He hurtled the handcuff key across the cell. Chelpinski's arm flopped to the floor next to his lifeless body. Gregorovitch knelt down and patted Chelpinski on the shoulder, whispering an emotional, *"Goodbye, my dear friend,"* before kissing him on the forehead. A borderline psychopath, it was the nearest that Gregorovitch had ever been to experiencing grief.

Standing up and hurrying across to the cell door, Gregorovitch swung it open and then stopped dead in his tracks. Standing there blocking the exit, hands on his hips and a face like thunder was a grim-faced President Baronovski, accompanied by several members of his heavily armed elite bodyguard.

A shocked Gregorovitch's bruised jaw dropped and he very nearly shat himself on the spot.

The President, glanced over Gregorovitch's shoulder at Chelpinsky's body, sighed and said, *"Ah, what a deeply touching scene. I see that General Chelpinsky has fallen down on the job - as usual! Now, Comrade Colonel, where might you be going in such a hurry? You had better explain yourself!"*

Standing rigidly to attention, Ivanski replied, *"I, er, the, er, the General has been taken ill, Comrade President. I was just going to summon medical assistance,"* said a panicking Gregorovitch. It was all he could think of to say.

Baronovitch nodded, "*Yes, I can see that he is not very well. In fact it looks to me as if he is quite dead, which is a great pity. I had such plans for him. Never mind, we'll just have to make do with you.*"

"*Oh, and before we proceed any further,*" the President continued, looking slowly around the cell, "*didn't you have an important prisoner in here for interrogation?*" Gregorovitch nodded, "*Yes, we did Mr President.*" The President raised an eyebrow, "*And?*"

A flustered Gregorovitch said, "*Well sir, this is going to sound a little left of field, but you see, er, a 'Time-Machine' arrived here in the cell with three men on board and they…*"

Baronovski laughed heartily then held his hand up to stop Gregorovitch speaking. Turning to his bodyguards and pointing at Chelpinski, he ordered, "*Gentlemen, remove that lump of meat,*" then pointing at the unfortunate Gregorovitch, instructed, "*after which I would like you to secure this miserable creature to the table. I need to have a word or two with him about what has really happened here today.*'

The Presidential Bodyguard rushed forward to do their master's bidding. Chelpinski was released from the remaining handcuff and dragged unceremoniously out of the cell before being dumped on the passage floor. The bodyguards returned then used the handcuffs to secure Gregorovitch firmly to the table.

The President removed his very expensive camel-hair overcoat, a present from Iran's President Mahmoud Ahmadinejad - just before he was ousted, and handed it to a bodyguard. Then he slowly began removing his leather gloves, easing them off one finger at a time. A silly thought raced through Ivanski's mind, *"He should be doing that in time to the music of 'The Stripper.'"* His face creased and he gave a nervous giggle.

"Something amuses you, my friend?" asked the President. Gregorovitch shook his head, *"No, Mister President."* Baronovski smiled and said, *"Good, because this is not a laughing matter - not for you anyway!"*
Flexing his fingers Baronovski said, *"Now then Colonel, you have some explaining to do. There is no need to give yourself any brain-strain, because I am going to help you find your way - but I must warn you that fairy stories about 'Time-Machines' just won't cut it with me!"* He shrugged his shoulders, *"Your President likes a joke as much as the next man, but today we are going to be very serious, you and I."*

"But Mister President, what I told you was the truth!" whined a desperate Gregorovitch. Ivan's mouth was now so dry that his top lip was stuck to his teeth. *"I beg you to believe me, sir. I am and always have been a loyal servant of the State. I even voted for you at the last election!"*

The President smirked, and replied, *"Colonel, you know as well as I do that votes don't count in Russian elections, so your protestations of undying loyalty are a complete waste of time. A man in your position should know better!"*

then picking up the surgical pincers, he glanced at them admiringly and said, *"I think that we'll make a start with these lovely things."*

Gregorovitch's stomach churned and he farted. He knew full well what was about to happen to him, he'd seen it done to others often enough. Sweating heavily, Gregorovitch stuttered, *"M, M, Mister President, there is no need for any of this. I will happily tell you all that I know."* The President looked at his watch and yawned, *"I know you will, eventually, but let's just have a little bit of fun first, shall we, my dear boy."*

Looking at Ivanski's hands, the President sighed, *"What long tapering fingers you have. I'm afraid that you'll never be able to use those to play the Balalaika again!"* *"But I don't play an instrument,"* wailed Gregorovitch. *"No matter,"* said the President, who was enjoying himself immensely.

Turning to one of his bodyguards, the President instructed him to, *"Grip him tightly will you!"* The bodyguard went behind Gregorovitch and gripped the top of his arms so that he couldn't wriggle.

The President then took hold of Gregorovitch's left hand and with consummate ease and one swift snip of the surgical pincers, lopped his little finger off. An agonised Gregorovitch screamed with pain as his body went rigid with shock.

"Not so nice when the glove is on the other hand, is it! I should have said when the shoe is on the other foot, but that will come later," said the President, roaring with laughter.

Gregorovitch whimpered as he glanced at the little finger that had been snipped from his hand and was laid in the middle of the table like a chipolata, then gazed in shock at the bleeding stump where the finger had been only a few seconds earlier. He was trembling uncontrollably.

"There, there, easy does it, Colonel," said the President, patting him paternally on the head, *"only another nine to go, then perhaps we'll make a start on your toes! By the way, I forgot to ask you, are you left or right handed? Not that it really matters now,"* the President tutted, *"and silly old me, look, I forgot to attached the battery wires to the pincers! I'd better heat them up and seal your wound. We don't want you getting an infection, do we. Well, not just yet anyway!"*

He connected the Surgical Pincers to the batteries, waited until the blades glowed then reached for Gregorovitch's bleeding hand. *"I'll just cauterise the stump if I may, then it's time for another finger or two, I think."*

Gregorovitch screamed in agony as the President pressed the bright red pincers against his bleeding stump, *"Noooooooo, I beg you! Aaaaaaaagh - you mu-dak!"* bellowed Gregorovitch (using a very rude Russian expletive).

The President smiled, shook his head sadly and said, "*It's no use you trying to sweet talk me, Gregorovitch!*" Turning to his bodyguard, the President said, "*Grip him tightly now. Time for the removal of another digit!*"

Gregorovitch fainted. The President tutted, "*Fetch a bucket of cold water,*" he ordered.

Ж

CHAPTER SEVENTEEN

'THE ZELNOGRAD MORTUARY'

Doctor Igor Bobrov, Senior Mortician at Forensic Bureau No 8, of the Municipal Hospital No 3, Zelnograd, turned to his ancient assistant, the doddery Leonid Voronin, and said *"Leonid, apparently we need to give those two new arrivals over there some priority, particularly that one on Table Number Two, the one wearing the fancy uniform,"* pointing at the corpse of the late General Chelpinski.

The Doctor lived for his work and often referred to the ungodly stench of the preservative formaldehyde that permeated every corner of the mortuary as being – *"Eu de Formaldehyde,"* much to the amusement of his long-suffering henchman, the spooky Leonid, who cackled dutifully every time the Doctor cracked a funny.

"As you can see, Leonid, those two were both senior officers in the FSB, although that's purely academic now," said the Doctor *"It doesn't really matter what they were in now, does it Doctor,"* replied Leonid, *"They're here to be diced and sliced just like the rest."*

"You have such a colourful way with words, Leonid," said Doctor Bobrov, *"I could not have put it better myself."*

Laid out on the table immediately adjacent to Chelpinski's was the bruised, battered and mutilated body of the late Colonel Ivanski Gregorovitch.

"The General, apparently, had taken poison and the Colonel died whilst under interrogation. His heart must have been weak. For some strange reason, our beloved President has taken a personal interest in knowing precisely what the poison was that took the General's life," said Doctor Bobrov, *"therefore his autopsy must take priority."*

The other one," he said, pointing at Gregorovitch's mangled corpse, *"the Colonel, is of no real consequence. His fingers, toes and testicles are inside that plastic bag tucked in between his legs.."*

Doctor Bobrov tutted, shook his head and said, *"Just look at that poor man's hands, Leonid."* Leonid yawned, exposing a mouth full of yellowing ancient and badly fitting false teeth, in between which were the remnants of that morning's breakfast, and replied, *"Once thing's for certain, Doctor, he'll never be able to scratch his arse again!"* He gave a bronchitic laugh then seeing Doctor Bobrov wasn't amused, decided that he'd better get on with the job.

I wonder what they did to deserve that sort of treatment?" asked Leonid. *"Ours not to reason why, Leonid - and it certainly doesn't do to ask,"* said Doctor Bobrov quietly.

"You might as well shove the Colonel straight into the 'fridge, Leonid," said the Doctor, *"it doesn't take the brains of an Archbishop to see the cause of his demise. There's no rush for him, he can go to the back of the queue."*

"Once you've done that, you'd better undress the General and prepare his body for autopsy. Don't cut any of his uniform off though, I'm sure that we'll be able to make good use of it. I will be back shortly to commence the autopsy. I just want to have a relaxing cigarette before I begin."

Leonid nodded and bowed his head respectfully as the Senior Mortician made his way out of the gloomy Mortuary. *"Those cigarettes will be the death of him,"* mumbled Leonid, *"Somebody'll be doing his autopsy one of these days!"*

Leonid looked down at the undamaged corpse of the General and thought, *"I wonder if this FSB swine has anything of value left on his person?"*

He slid the cuffs of Chelpinski's jacket sleeves back and saw to his delight that the General was still wearing an expensive wristwatch. *"Huh they missed the watch. Well, that'll do for starters,"* thought Leonid, unfastening the watch and examining it. *"A Rolex!"* he mumbled, *"I'm definitely having that!"* slipping it into the gore-stained pocket of his once white coverall. He then decided to carry out a quick search of the General's trouser pockets.

Disappointingly, he found only a few kopek coins, a handkerchief and a comb in the General's trouser pockets, so decided to roll the corpse over and search his back pockets to see if there was a wallet or a bill-fold tucked away. Grabbing hold of the General's shoulder he rolled him over from his back onto his front.

Without any warning, the General suddenly turned and sat up. Gasping with shock, Leonid stepped back, his jaw dropping in surprise. Chelpinski raised his arm and used his elbow to strike the shocked old Assistant Mortician a vicious blow to his Adam's apple, cutting off his oxygen.

Turning purple, Voronin sank down onto his knees then slowly fell onto his back, his spindly fingers clawing at his throat as he fought to draw breath into his shattered old larynx.

Chelpinski leapt off the table, kicked Voronin in the face then stamped viciously several times on his throat. Leonid died very quietly and very quickly.

Always planning ahead, General Chelpinski had cleverly faked his own death by using a drug that mirrored the effects of potassium cyanide and gave off a similar odour of almonds but was not fatal. The effects of the drug he had taken, he knew, would wear off after a couple of hours and with a bit of luck he could then make good his escape.

In Russia, those in elevated positions of authority, like Chelpinsky, always had a 'Plan B' tucked away in the far reaches of their minds in the event of things going badly wrong for them, as they often did in Russia, particularly for those in positions of importance. If your career went bad then that was the end of it. As the President was fond of saying, *"You can't reheat a souffle!"*

When things had gone so badly wrong for him in the Lubyanka Prison, Chelpinski knew that his time in the sun was up and that there would be no going back. He'd decided there and then that the time had definitely come to activate his 'Plan B' and make good his escape.

Realising that he now had only had a few minutes before the Senior Mortician returned, Chelpinsky quickly undressed Voronin and then took his own uniform off and changed into Voronin's clothes. Although not a perfect fit, fortunately both men were of a similar size.

He dressed Voronin in his General's uniform and then lifted the old man's still warm body onto the autopsy table before covering it with a bloodied sheet that had been covering a nearby traffic accident corpse on an adjacent marble table. It would have to do for the moment.

Turning and looking down sorrowfully at the battered body of Ivanski, Chelpinski whispered, *"I promise you that I will seek revenge on those bastards that did this, Ivanski - and I give you my word that those so-called 'Time-Travellers' will also get what's coming to them."*

Chelpinsky glanced around the mortuary, *"Now, regrettably I must leave you here in this hell-hole along with the rest of these unfortunates. Goodbye old friend,"* he said, patting Gregorvitch's shoulder affectionately.

He picked up the few personal items that Voronin had stolen, including his watch, and stuffed them into his trouser pockets. *"Thieving old swine!"* he said, spitefully punching Leonid in the ribs.

As Chelpinsky walked over towards the Mortuary door, suddenly and without warning the door handle turned noisily and the door was pushed open.

Using the back of the door as cover, Chelpinski ducked behind it and hid, then swiftly side-stepped out of the Mortuary as the door swung closed, luckily without the incoming Doctor Igor Bobrov spotting him.

Doctor Bobrov had returned after having his cigarette and taking a hefty slug of vodka from the hip flask that he always carried. He found that these days the vodka helped him to relax and also stopped his hands from trembling.

Seeing that other than the dead bodies, the Mortuary was empty and his assistant Leonid was nowhere to be seen, Bobrov tutted and called out, *"Leonid, you pox-ridden old rascal! Where are you?"*

Bobrov looked across at the covered corpse on Autopsy Table No 2 and was puzzled. He tutted, *"Why on earth has he placed a bloodied sheet over the General's body, I wonder?"* He tutted, and said angrily, *"That will cause cross-contamination if we are not careful."*

Walking over to the autopsy table and pulling back the sheet, he gasped and stepped back in surprise when he saw who lay underneath it. Leonid's lifeless, rheumy eyes stared blankly up into space.

After a moment Doctor Bobrov smiled and wagged a nicotine stained finger at his assistant, *"Leonid, you old rascal, how many times have I told you not to play games with me. My heart won't take it. Now get up off the slab and let us begin our work, comrade."*

Leonid, of course, didn't move. *"Come along, Leonid,"* said a now irate Bobrov, *"the joke has gone far enough, let us waste no more time. There is much to be done!"*

Leonid laid there, his unseeing eyes gazing upwards at the ceiling, a rictus grimace on his face. Drawing the sheet further back, Bobrov noticed the catastrophic damage done to Leonid's throat and gasped. *"Leonid, what has happened here?.."*

He dropped the sheet back onto Leonid's face then turned and ran towards the telephone to summon assistance.

Outside the Mortuary, Chelpinski waited until it was quiet then slipped out of the unmanned side-entrance of the Municipal Clinical Hospital No 3. He knew that he had to get away from the area and out of central Moscow as soon as possible before the alarm was raised. The hospital would soon be crawling with police investigators and the FSB, wanting to know what had happened to General Chelpinski's corpse.

He had much to do and the first thing Chelpinsky wanted to do was to change out of the old Mortuary Assistants ill-fitting suit. It stank of stale tobacco, body odour, piss and the disconcerting whiff of what Chelpinski recognised as being formaldehyde.

Chelpinski had checked Igor's pockets to see if there was any cash there, which apart from the few kopeks that he'd stolen from Chelpinsky in the first place, there wasn't much else. The general had a small amount of money in his wallet, but that had been stolen by one of the ambulance attendants on the way to the mortuary.

Other than that, Chelpinski's wallet had been empty, apart from his all-important FSB identity card. Like royalty, he normally didn't carry cash about with him; he never needed to. His left-hand man Gregorovitch had always seen to that sort of thing.

He would have to make his way on foot to the secret alternative accommodation that he had maintained for a number of years. Chelpinsky called it his 'E.B.O.P. Loc,' (Emergency Bug Out Procedure Location). It was so secret that not even Gregorovitch had known about it.

The hidey-hole was tucked away in a nondescript block of flats on the outskirts of Moscow. Disconcertingly, it was quite some distance away. Cursing roundly, Chelpinski pulled his coat collar up as it started to rain. He knew that it was going to take him hours to walk to his E.B.O.P. location on the other side of Moscow.

Head down, he shuffled along slowly, adopting an old man's doddering gait; people noticed you more when you rushed and the last thing that Chelpinski wanted was to be noticed.

In the distance he could hear police sirens. He turned down a side street and gradually lengthened his pace.

Chelpinski was seething; everything had gone so terribly wrong for him. *'Those bastards"* in the 'Time-Team' were to blame and he was determined that he would get revenge.

Ж

CHAPTER EIGHTEEN

'SO – WHAT'S NEXT?'

It was a quiet Sunday afternoon and close friends Mike Fraser and Graham St Anier were sat inside the old 'Dog and Duck Coaching Inn' in Beverley having a leisurely post-Sunday Dinner ale or two, just chatting amiably and simply taking pleasure in the delightful ambience of the establishment.

The Dog and Duck Inn, one of the ever diminishing traditional English hostelries, never disappointed. Mike and Graham loved it there and it was their favourite watering-hole. The friendly and welcoming Landlord kept a fine cellar and for those fortunate enough to get a table, the food was unfailingly first class, value for money and, all-importantly, filling.

'The Dog and Duck Inn'

Graham leaned back in his carver chair and took a refreshing swig of his favourite ale, Timothy Taylor's 'Boltmakers.' After wiping the moustache of luxurious creamy white foam from his top lip he said, *"By gum, it's a nice drop of stuff is that. Nectar of the Gods!"*

Mike sipping his own beer, nodded in agreement. Graham said,*" Well Mike, you can't deny it lad, we've had some cracking experiences travelling through time with Ed De Jong, haven't we?"*

Mike nodded, *"Aye, we certainly have, my friend - and we've made a ridiculous amount of money in the process. It thrills me to bits to think that we won't ever have to raise a pinkie again if we dinnae want tae."*

Graham nodded, *"Speaking as a blue-blooded very careful Yorkshireman, often unfairly referred to as being 'a bit of a nipscrew,' I have to agree with you, we are definitely living the dream!"*

Graham smiled and continued, *"You know, as I've said before, my favourite 'Time-Travel' visit was when we transported back to Paris in 1793. That was absolutely brilliant - a bit scary at times, but what an adventure. We saw so much and we met so many interesting people."*

"Aye, and we bumped into the odd toe-rag as well!" said Mike, *"Remember old Maximilien Robespierre, Graham? What a wee jobby he was. A real piece of work!"* *"I certainly do, and he certainly was"* said Graham.

"Still, he got his just desserts in the end, eh!" said Mike. Graham nodded in agreement, *"Aye, the old short back and sides, courtesy of Madame Guillotine!"* blanching as he remembered the whoosh and thud of the guillotine blade that had parted Robespierre's head from his body.

"Suppose we all have a particularly favourite 'Time-Travel' visit," said Graham, *"What's yours, Mike?"*

Pausing for a moment to think about it, Mike replied, *"Och, if truth be known, I've enjoyed them all pal, but it was great fun travelling forwards in time to visit Hull in 2119 and being able to see what happened there after World War 3 had been declared."*

"It's so interesting to see what lays ahead, although we'll never be able to tell anyone about it. Official Secrets Act and all that cack," said Mike. *"Makes you wonder just what else is around the corner. We're all doomed!"* said Graham gloomily. *"Is it being so cheerful that keeps you going?"* asked Mike.

Graham nodded in agreement then, brightening up, asked, *"So, where are we off to next then, or is it high time that the old 'Time-Travel' team had a good rest and we just sit back and enjoy the fruits of our labours?"*

Leaning back in his chair, Mike said, *"It may surprise you to know, Graham, that I have recently been cogitating on precisely that very subject. We're obviously so loaded that we don't need to go thrashing around seeking treasure or anything like that, but I would like to have just one more crack at something really 'historical' before I hang up my 'Time-Travel' boots."*

"*Something really historical? Now that sounds a bit intriguing,*" said Graham. "*Tell you what,*" said Mike, "*you go and get us a refill and then when you return I'll tell you all about where and when I'm thinking of going to next.*"

"*Give me a little clue first!*" said Graham.

"*Well, this might sound a wee strange for a lapsed Presbyterian, but I would like to pay a visit to Jerusalem and Bethlehem during the period A.D. 36 - or thereabouts,*" said Mike. "*A.D. 36! Jerusalem and Bethlehem! Seriously?*" said Graham Mike nodded, "*Aye, seriously.*"

"*So why then and there, dare I ask?*" said Graham. "*I'd like to try and find out what really happened to either the Ark of the Covenant or the Holy Grail.*" replied Mike.

Graham tutted, "*"Oh, not those two hoary old chestnuts. We all know that the Ark of the Covenant is tucked away in that church in Ethiopia and the Holy Grail is supposed to be hidden somewhere in Wales.*" said Graham. "*Och, well I'm not convinced,*" said Mike, "*and I'd like to find out the truth for myself. You can beat and egg, you can beat a drum, but you cannae beat a good challenge!*"

Graham said, "*A.D. 36. Have you thought about what you'd do if you bumped into the man himself?*"

"Which man?" asked Mike. *"The big J C!"* said Graham, *"He was knocking around there at that time and it's not that big a place."* Mike shook his head, *"To be honest, I hadnae given that any thought,"* said Mike.

Picking up the empty pint glasses Graham said, *"Well perhaps you should. I'll go and get the beers in whilst you do a bit more cogitating,"* and headed off for the bar.

Calling after him, Mike said, *"Aye, well you're a long time looking at the inside of a lid, Graham, so I'd just like to see for myself if there's any truth in the matter."*

As Graham headed towards the bar, easing his way past the crowded tables, the Inn door opened and a stooped middle-aged man walked in. Graham glanced at him.

Although the man was wearing spectacles and sporting a bushy moustache, Graham thought for just a moment that he recognised him, but he couldn't for the life of him place from where. Nevertheless, he smiled at the man, who nodded and smiled back at him.

The mystery man then went and stood behind Graham at the bar and when it was his turn to be served asked quietly for, *"A Smirnoff vodka, neat, please, Landlord."*

Glancing surreptitiously up at the mirror behind the bar, the man spotted Mike Fraser sat over in the corner of the Inn leafing through *'The Digger'* his favourite crime magazine that he had sent down regularly from Glasgow.

Graham had by that time returned to the table, clutching two precious pints of Yorkshire's finest beer, without spilling a drop of the precious liquid.

The man at the bar could hear Graham saying, *"Well, Mike, we could always go and pay Nostradamus a visit, I've always fancied that." "Why Nostradamus?"* asked Mike. *"He might be able to tell us the winner of the William Hill Brontë Cup at York races next week,"* said Graham, winking at him. They both laughed.

The mystery man threw the vodka down his throat, coughed, then whispered to himself, *"At long last. Mister St Anier and Mister Fraser. Now I will have two hares with one shot."* The Landlord smiled at the man and asked him, *"Sorry, did you say something, sir?"* Chelpinsky replied, *"Yes, I'd like another vodka please." "Certainly sir, coming right up!"* said the ever cheerful Landlord.

Glancing across at Chelpinski, Graham said to Mike, *"You know what, Mike, I'm sure I know that geezer at the bar. There's summat very familiar about him, but I can't quite put my finger on it."*

"Well, go and offer to buy him a drink and why not ask him to come and join us if you're that concerned," said Mike. *"You're right, Mike, I'll go and do just that. I don't want to offend anybody!"* said Graham.

Ж

CHAPTER NINETEEN

'NO PLACE LIKE HOME'

"And so, er, we were just wondering if you'd care to come and join us?" Graham said to the mystery man.

Patting Graham on the shoulder, the man replied, *"That's very kind of you, I'd love to,"* thinking to himself, *"Ha, they've played right into my hands, the idiots!"*

"Look, let me buy you a drink and then I'll introduce you to my friend, Mike," said Graham. *"I'm Graham St Anier, by the way."* The man smiled and shook hands with Graham.

"What's your poison?" asked Graham. The man started, *"I beg your pardon?"* he asked. *"What's your poison, what are you drinking?"* *"Oh, er, vodka please,"* replied Chelpinski. *"Is that a straight vodka, or would you like something with it?"* *"No thank you, just straight vodka,"* said Chelpinski.

Graham ordered fresh drinks then the two of them walked across the pub and sat down alongside Mike.

The stranger held out his hand, *"How do you do, sir."* Mike smiled and shook the man's hand, *"Well hello there, I'm Mike Fraser. Sorry, I didn't catch your name?"*

Smiling disarmingly the man replied, *"That's because I didn't give it,"* he said. *"What have we got here?"* thought Mike.

"Like Graham, I'm sure I know your face frae somewhere?" said Mike, looking puzzled. *"Well then, perhaps I'd better put you out of your misery and introduce myself,"* said the man. *"Be rude not to, cocker,"* said Graham.

Removing his glasses, and peeling his false moustache off, the man said, *"My name is Igor Chelpinski, late of the Russian FSB."*

Mike started, gave an involuntary gasp, then said, *"My God, Graham, it's Chelps!"* *"Bloody hell fire - and I've just bought him a pigging drink!"* said Graham. Mike started to stand up.

"Sit down, Scotlander! I should warn you both," said Chelpinski, keeping his voice low, *"I am carrying a pistol in my pocket - and I will not hesitate to use it!"* Mike was flushed with anger, *"Well, Chelps, if you're lucky you're only going to get one of us!"*

"I said sit down! I won't tell you again!" hissed Chelpinski. *"Better do as he says, Mike. We don't want*

anyone else getting injured," said Graham. A reluctant and furious looking Mike sat down.

Chelpinski smiled, *"That's much better, my Scottish friend." "I'm no friend of yours, Chelps!"* said a seething Mike, *"for two pins I'd knock your bloody block off!"*

Chelpinski continued, *"Just so that you are aware. The fully loaded pistol I'm holding in my pocket is an MP-443 Grach which, knowing your background, I'm sure you're familiar with, gentlemen."*

"In case you aren't, let me tell you that it fires 17 high capacity, semi-armour piercing bullets and can do a great deal of damage. So, make any more foolish moves and I assure you that I'll use all of them. There's plenty for you two," Chelpinski looked around the Inn, *"and enough for the rest of the customers in here!"*

"You bloody miserable little toe-rag!" said Graham. Chelpinski smiled, *"Thank you for the compliment,"* he replied.

"So, Chelps, what's the plot then?" asked Mike. "The plot?" queried Chelpinsky. "What are you doing here in Beverley. You obviously haven't come to look at the Minster?" said Mike. "And more importantly, why have you sought us two out?" said Graham.

The ingratiating smile vanished from Chelpinsky's face and he said quietly, *"I am here because amongst others, whom have already been dealt with incidentally, I hold you both responsible for the death of my very dear friend Colonel Ivanski Gregorovitch and of course for the damage you did to my career in the FSB, so I made a promise to myself that you would not go unpunished - no matter how long it took."*

Mike tutted, *"Old Gregory Peckski has docked his clogs then. Oh dear, how sad, never mind!"*

Chelpinski glared at Mike, *"It is not a matter to be treated with such flippancy, Scotsman. Ivanski was a very dear comrade of mine and I promised myself that I would deal personally with those responsible for his untimely death."*

"Why are you getting pear-shaped with us two? We didn't top him!" asked Graham.

"I know that you didn't," said Chelpinski, *"but you were partially responsible, so you must also be punished!" "Just as a matter of interest, who did see him off the side then?"* asked Mike. *"If you must know, it was President Baronovski himself!"* said Chelpinski.

"Well," sighed Graham, *"if you're gonna go, you might as well be helped on your way by the main man!" "I will not warn either of you again, Mr St Anier, it is not a joking matter!"* said Chelpinski, *"Ivanski was a close friend and comrade." "Fortunes of war, dear chap. If you put your head above the parapet, you risk getting your head blown off,"* said Mike.

Just at that moment a loud shout came from behind the bar, *"Time - Ladies and Gentlemen - please! Drink up! Let's have yer glasses "* Everyone looked across at the bar where the Landlord was placing a tea-towel across the beer pumps.

"Och, that's a bloody shame," said Mike, *"we've got to go,"* he tutted, *"Just as the party was getting started."* *"So, what happens now, Chelpinski?"* asked Graham, *"You've obviously got something up your sleeve."* Mike nodded, *"Aye, it's that bloody MP-443 Grach!"*

"I have decided that you are going to take me to your offices in Kingswood." Graham interrupted him, *"My, you have been doing your homework."* *"Interrupt me again and you will regret it!"* threatened Chelpinski, then continued, *"Then you are going to 'fly' me to the Kremlin in your 'Time-Machine' where I am going to take out President Baronovski,"* said Chelpinsky *"Take him oot, what, like tae a dance you mean?"* asked Mike.

"I do not understand the nuances of your very clunky language, Mr Fraser, so let me make it quite clear to you. You two are going to take me to Moscow in your 'Time-Machine and then I am going to shoot the President," said Chelpinsky, *"By executing Baronovski and dealing with the two of you I will have kept the promise I made to Ivanski."*

Mike nodded, *"Och, right, nae problem there then. We just pop across tae Kingswood, jump inside the 'T3-Travellator, crank it up then nip across time to the*

Kremlin and top the Russian President. Sounds like an excellent plan tae me."

"And you mentioned us two? What've you got planned for us?" asked Graham. "Aye, do tell. I'm intrigued," said Mike.

"What I propose to do initially," said Chelpinsky, *" is to leave one of you behind with the President in his office, both dead of course, to take the blame, then the one of you that survives can fly my to a place of my choosing, after which I'll let you go on your way. You have my word on that."*

"Your word! Och, well that's as good as money in the bank tae me, you being an officer and a gentleman of the FSB" said Mike, adding, *"You ken what, Chelps old bean, I wouldnae trust you as far as I could throw you!"*

At that precise moment the pub doors swung open and a man's voice called out, *"Taxi for Mr Fraser!"*

A smiling Chelpinski said, *"Ah, fortune favours the brave. We have transport, gentlemen!"* "Huh, brave my arse," said Graham, *"you slink in here like a thief in the night and threaten these innocent people then have the nerve to call yourself brave! You're nowt but a little turd!"*

Chelpinski glared at Graham *"I would advise you to shut your mouth, you are beginning to get on my nerves!"* *"Leave it Graham,"* said Mike, *"we'd better do as he says. Come on!"* Mike and Graham knocked their beers back then stood up to leave. *"Waste not, want not, eh Chelps!"* said Mike. *"Move!"* ordered Chelpinski.

They walked towards the pub doors, Mike and Graham leading, Chelpinski behind them. As they left the 'Dog and Duck' Chelpinski turned and called out cheerfully to the Landlord, *"Thank you my friend, see you next week, maybe!"* *"Thank you, take care, sir!"* replied the Landlord.

The three men left the pub and climbed into the waiting taxi, which was parked immediately outside the Inn. Graham and Chelpinski sat in the rear seat, Mike sat next to the driver.

Mike turned to Chelpinski and asked, *"Where to?"* *"Your offices, of course,"* replied Chelpinski. *"Kingswood Retail Park, please driver, and dinnae spare the horses"* said Mike gruffly. *"Oh, don't you want to go to Leconfield first to drop your friend off, that's the usual procedure, sir?"* said the polite taxi driver.

Glancing in his rear-view mirror the driver said, *"Oh, and I only expected the two of you."* *"Kingswood Retail Park! Just drive, pal!"* said Mike grumpily. *"You're paying the fare, sir,"* replied the driver. Pointing over his shoulder at Chelpinski, Mike replied, *"No I'm not - he is!"*

Ж

CHAPTER TWENTY

'CHEERIO CHELPINSKI'

"Right, so here we are, inside the hallowed portals of the Kremlin - now what?" said Mike stepping out of the 'T3-Travellator' closely followed by Graham. Chelpinski, bringing up the rear, snapped, *"Now we wait!"* He was clearly on edge. *"Wait for what, precisely?"* asked Graham. *"For the arrival of our beloved President Baronovski,"* said Chelpinski. *"Huh, he's not my beloved President,"* said Graham.

"How do you know he's going to put in an appearance, Chelps?" asked Mike.

Chelpinski glanced down at his wristwatch, *"Because President Baronovski is very much a creature of habit - I emphasise the word 'creature' - and he will arrive here in approximately ten minutes, give or take a few seconds either way."*

Gazing around the presidential office, Mike commented, *"Nice little luxury pad he has here, eh,"* he said, *"must have cost the workers a few roubles!"* Chelpinski waved his pistol, *"Shut up! We Russians will not take any lectures from you capitalist swines. Now, both of you, over there and sit down!"*

"*Och, you're such a sensitive wee soul,*" said Mike. "*Move!*" said Chelpinski, "*I will not tell you again!*" "*What, onto that wee plush banquette?*" said Mike. Chelpinski nodded. "*Say please, Chelps!*" said Graham.

"*Just move yourselves - and stop calling me Chelps, it is most disrespectful and I do not like it!*" said Chelpinski, pointing his pistol directly at Graham. "*My God, you're a bit touchy this morning. The old 'Farmer Giles' playing you up, Chelps?*" said Graham defiantly.

As ordered, Mike and Graham went and made themselves comfortable on the richly upholstered banquette. "*Very plush this,*" said Mike, "*It's like one of those love seats at the cinema!*" "*Aye, well don't get any ideas, you're not my type,*" said Graham.

Meanwhile, Chelpinski had slunk across the office and was standing behind the office doors, so that when they eventually swung open he'd be well out of sight when the Presdient entered.

Mike turned to Graham and whispered, "*Och, we're both in the same boat here pal, and it's sinking fast!*" Graham nodded in agreement, "*What the hell are we going to do now?*" he asked. "*Stop talking you two!*" ordered Chelpinsky.

They sat quietly and waited. In the background, the only sounds that could be heard - the ominous ticking of Hitler's ormeleau clock and Graham's stomach, rumbling.

After a few minutes, outside the office doors they heard the sound of approaching footsteps and several voice chatting animatedly. Chelpinski waved his pistol and hissed, *"Quickly you two, off the banquette and get down behind the President's desk - keep out of sight!"*

As Graham and Mike hid behind the desk, the room doors swung open and President Baronovski strode into his office. Once inside, the doors swung shut behind him. He sauntered cockily across to the banquette, throwing his very expensive overcoat and a finely tooled briefcase carelessly onto it.

Turning around, he started to yawn but stopped when he saw Mike and Graham crouched down behind his desk. *"What is this?"* he roared, reaching inside his jacket for the pistol that he had tucked in a shoulder holster.

From behind him, Chelpinsky called out, *"Don't try anything stupid, Mister President!"* Turning to look at Chelpinski, the President's jaw dropped in shock as he recognised him.

A puzzled Baronovski froze mometarily, then recovering his composure, said, *"General Chelpinski, or should I say ex-General Chelpinski - what an unpleasant surprise - it's really you!"*

Chelpinski smiled and replied, *"Yes it is. Well spotted, Mister President - sharp as ever I see!"* Pointing at Graham and Mike, Baronovski asked, *"What is going on here, and who are those two thugs, skulking beneath my desk - assassins I suppose?"*

"Just shut up, oh - and move your hand away from your pistol!" ordered Chelpinski. Baronovski removed his hand from inside his jacket. *"You will pay for this outrage, you insolent swine. You know as well as I do that it is a capital offence to threaten me!"* spluttered Baronovski. .

Chelpinski strode quickly across the office then, without any warning, used the barrel of his pistol to strike the President in the mouth. Baronovski gasped then sank to his knees, clutching his badly split lips, the bright red blood dribbling through his fingers, staining his immaculate white Italian silk shirt,

"You have broken my front teeth, you bastard!" mumbled Baronovski.

"Save your breath, Mister President, that's only the beginning - and like you, your teeth are false. You needn't concern yourself, however, because you won't be needing teeth where you're going!" said a smiling Chelpinski.

Turning towards Mike and Graham Chelpinsky waved his pistol at them and said, *"You two, help the President onto his throne - he isn't feeling very well!"*

Mike and Graham helped the shocked President to his feet and gently lowered him into his chair. Then, pointing at the banquette, Chelpinsky ordered them to, *"Now get back over there!"*

Mike and Graham walked over to the luxurious seat and sat down. "*On the banquette! Off the banquette! I wish he'd make his bloody mind up!*" said Graham.

Chelpinsky sat on the side of the President's desk and said to Baronovski, "*Incidentally, Mister President, if you make any attempt to press the panic button that I know is hidden underneath your desk, I will shoot you much sooner than I intended!*"

Baronovski glared at him, "*You don't scare me, you chicken shit! If you're going to shoot me then you'd better get on with it!*" he said.

Chelpinski leaned over and placed the barrel of his MP-443 Grach pistol against the President's left temple, making him flinch, "*As you wish. Any final words of wisdom for posterity before I blow your brains out, Mister President - and I use the term 'brains' loosely?*" asked Chelpinski.

Through broken teeth, Baronovitch mumbled, "*Why are you doing this to me, Chelpinski? Have you forgotten, it was I that made you a General?*" A bitter Chelpinski said, "*Yes, that is true, but you also snatched everything away from me, just like that!*" clicking his fingers. Shrugging, he continued, "*But you know I could have lived with that. What was worse, much worse in my eyes, was that you personally tortured and then slaughtered my oldest and dearest friend for no reason other than your own entertainment.*"

"Oh, and which friend was that? I can't imagine that you have very many!" lisped Baronovski. *"Colonel Ivanski Gregorovitch!"* said Chelpinski.

"Oh, Ivanski Gregorovitch!" said Baronovski, voice whistling through his broken teeth, *"Yes, I remember him well. His was not a particularly impressive departure from this world. As I recall, he squealed like a stuck pig and begged me for mercy before he folded!"*

Mike whispered to Graham, *"Oh dear, that hasnae gone down too well with Chelps. Would you look at the face on him!"*

A white-faced and enraged Chelpinski shouted, *"You swine!"* then leaned across the desk and raked the sharp foresight of his pistol down the President's cheek, ripping the flesh open, before striking him a wicked blow on the side of his temple with the pistol butt.

Mike and Graham both flinched at the obscene 'clunking' sound from pistol as it bounced off the President's skull. *"Och, that's going tae sting in the morning,"* said Mike. *"Serves him right!"* replied an unsympathetic Graham.

The battered Baronovski gave a grunt then fell face-down onto his desk, smashing his nose in the process. He laid there dazed, blood dripping from his torn mouth, ripped cheek, and now broken nose, the blood from all three wounds pooling out onto the previously pristine Presidential blotting pad. Baronovski wasn't having a very good start to his day.

Turning to Mike and Graham, Chelpinski said, *"Now, gentlemen, the choice is yours. You need to decide which one of you will die today alongside this creature, and who who will escape with me in the 'T3-Travellator.'*

"Ah," said Graham, *"so one of us is to be the fall-guy then?"* Chelpinski nodded, *"Yes, you see, I want the FSB to think that it was the Brits who did this to their beloved President. Obviously I will also double-tap Baronovski before I leave here so that he can't tell them otherwise,"* he smiled, *"Just think of the ructions that is going to cause, eh!"*

"You conniving little bugger!" said Graham. Chelpinski snarled, *"That's enough! Decide now who is coming with me and who is to remain here!"*

Mike said, *"Well, as we dinnae have a short straw tae draw, how's about we toss a coin for it, Graham?"* said Mike, winking at Graham. *"Aye, that'll do for me, cocker,"* replied Graham.

After tapping his pockets, Mike said, *"Er, could you see your way to lending me a coin please, Chelps, I seem to have left my money back at base?"*

Chelpinski sighed, *"Does your English friend not have a coin?"* he asked. Graham shook his head, *"No, I'm a bit like our Queen, I don't carry cash on my person. We try to avoid that sort of profligate behaviour where I come from in Yorkshire!"*

Chelpinski tutted then put his hand into his trouser pocket to find a coin. Having found one, he called out, "Here!" flipping a kopek up into the air, spinning it towards Mike - which was a big mistake.

When Mike stood up and reached out to catch the coin, he suddenly did a quick rugby-style feint and hurtled himself at the unsuspecting Chelpinski, punching him squarely on the jaw - landing one of the finest, meatiest left-hooks that Graham had seen for a long time. Chelpinski briefly whimpered then slid to the floor, unconscious.

"By hell, that was snorter, Mike. Look at Chelps, he's folded like a pack of cards," said Graham. Mike, rubbing his knuckles, smiled and said, *"Aye, well if you want a job doing properly, ask a soldier!"*

Chelpinski was spread out like a field of lettuice on the lush Presidential carpet, his pistol laid next to him. Mike leant down and picked it up, *"I'll hang on tae this wee beastie for now. Might come in handy later on,"* he said.

At that precise moment, the battered and bruised President Baronovski groaned, lifted his head up from the desk and mumbled something unintelligible, then pointed a trembling finger across the office. *"What's he blathering on about?"* asked Mike. *"I think he wants something to drink,"* said Graham.

Mike looked across the office to where Baronovski was pointing and saw a side-table with several crystal decanters full of various liquids, one of which was labelled Cognac. *"I'm slipping, I didn't notice that before. I'll go and pour him one,"* said Graham *"Could you get me a wee dram whilst you're at it!"* said Mike, *"I'm gagged."* Graham nodded.

"We'd better get a move on though, Graham. I'm sure that El Presidente here will have pressed the button under his desk and the 7th Russian Cavalry will be arriving here at any second to mount a rescue!" said Mike. Graham nodded.

Mike patted the President's shoulders sympathetically, *"Well, well, you have been in the wars, haven't you, Mister President. Still, dinnae worry your wee self, you'll have reinforcements clamouring to get in here before you can say Boris Yeltsin!"*

Graham returned carrying two large glasses of cognac and handed one to Mike. Just as Graham was about to take a sip from the glass he was clutching, Baronvski mumbled, *"Please, I beg you, give me a drink!"* *"Are you sure you want cognac? I don't think you'll be able to manage it with that mangled gob of yours?"* said Graham. The President nodded and replied, *"Let me be the judge of that!"*

Graham passed his glass to the President who then took a healthy slug of the cognac, grimacing as he swished it around his wounded gums and lips. "*I warned you, cocker!*" said an unsympathetic Graham.

Lurching to his feet the President staggered over to the unconscious Chelpinski then booted him in the face as hard as he could, saying, "*Zho-pa!*" an uncomplimentary Russian swear word. Chelpinski, totally out for the count, didn't feel a thing, but certainly would when he resurfaced. His jaw now jutted out at a strange angle and it looked very much as if it was broken or at the very least dislocated.

"*Oy, Baronovski - that's enough of that nonsense!*" said Mike, "*the poor wee fellow is defenceless!*" "*Aye, and you're not in the Lubyanka cells now, pal!*" added Graham. "*Go and sit yourself down before I knock you down !*" Mike said to the President.

Mumbling obscenities, the President tottered back to his desk, sat down heavily, took another slug of cognac from his glass, then howled in pain again. "*A wee glutton for punishment, eh!*" said Mike. "*It is medicinal*," replied the President, dabbing at his split lips with a handkerchief.

Turning to Graham, Mike said "*Right, well we'd better decide what we're going to do to these two reprobates.*" "*Let's just tie them both up and leave them here to sort themselves out*," said Graham.

"*Someone's bound to come looking for the President - and when they see what's happened to him, our mate Chelps here will definitely be for the high-jump,*" said Mike. "*No *sympathy whatsoever, they're both a pair of toe-rags!"* said Graham.

"OK, better tie them up and then we'll leg it in the 'T3.' said Mike. *"Let's put them both over there on the banquette, then they can have a friendly little chat whilst they're waiting to be released,"* said Graham, *"that's if Chelps can get his jaw working."*

"Good idea, Graham," said Mike, *"We'll use their belts and ties to secure them. That'll keep them out of harm's way whilst we get the 'T-3' sorted."*

A light on the President's desk suddenly flickered and there was the sound of a buzzer, followed by a sharp rapping on the outside of the office door. *"Here we go,"* said Mike, *"someone's after getting in here. We'd better crack on."*

They helped the President out of his chair and steered him across to the banquette, before removing his belt and tie, using them to fasten him to the banquette. After they'd done that, they lifted a groggy Chelpinsky up off the floor and did the same with him.

Mike looked at them both, sighed theatrically and said, *"Och, isnae that cute, the two of them look just like the 'Babes in the Wood!"*

As they headed for the 'T-3' Graham paused. *"What's the matter pal?"* asked Mike. *"I was just thinking, I'd like a little memento of our visit here,"* said Graham. *"Well you'd better be quick, the clock's ticking!"* replied Mike. Graham smiled, *"That's it! What a segue! I'm having Hitler's bloody clock!"*

He nipped across to the heavy ormoleau clock, picked it up and carried across to the 'T3-Travellator.' *"Hell fire, it weighs a bloody ton. It'll look grand on the mantlepiece at home though,"* said Graham.

A furious Baronovski called out, *"You have no right to take that, Englishman! That clock once belonged to Adolf Hitler and it now belongs to the Russian people. It is a war trophy!"*

"Oh, bog off, Baronovski!" said Graham, *"It belongs to me now! My very own war trophy!" "That is grand theft,"* shouted the President. *"What's your problem, pal - that's exactly how your lot got it in the first place!"* said Graham, *"Anyway, shut up and give your plastics a rest!"*

Mike and Graham jumped inside the 'T3-Travellator,' laid the clock onto one of the seats then sat in theirs. After they'd fastened their own safety belts, Graham said, *"Come on then, crank the old girl up Mike and let's get out of this madhouse before anything else happens." "No sooner said than done,"* said Mike, his fingers expertly dancing across several of the bewildering array of buttons and switches on the 'T-3's' complex console.

As the door of the 'T-3' was closing, Graham looked out and saw that Chelpinski had regained consciousness and was sitting up, struggling with his bindings. Graham waved and shouted, *"Cheerio Chelps!"* and Mike called out, *"TTFN Chelps!"* Within a few seconds the 'T3' had materialised and vanished into the ether, carrying its two passengers off to safety and well out of harms way.

Back on the banquette, a dazed Chelpinski's eyelids fluttered and he looked at the President through confused and bleary eyes, desperately trying to recall what had happened to him. After a moment or two his eyes focussed and he remembered what had occurred. He tried to stand up, but couldn't because the lads had fastened him firmly to the banquette with his tie and belt.

"Ah, I see that you are back in the land of the living, Chelpinski," said the President, *"but not for long, I can assure you!"* *"I think that my jaw is dislocated, Mr President,"* mumbled Chelpinski.

"That, my friend," said the President, *"is going to be the very least of your problems."* As he was speaking, the doors leading into the Presidential office swung open and several of his hefty body-guards rushed in, waving their weapons.

"Put your weapons away and release me immediately, then send for my personal physician, oh, and arrest this son of a dog sat next to me!" shouted Baronovski, nodding towards Chelpinski, and ordered, *"Take him straight to the Lubyanka Prison!"*

"What about my jaw?" whimpered Chelpinski. *"What about it?"* asked the President. *"I need medical*

treatment! It is dislocated or maybe even broken!" said Chelpinski. *"We'll leave it as it is for now. And anyway, it will save me a little time later on,"* said a smirking Baronovski.

The President turned to the head of his bodyguard detachment, *"Vladimir, make sure that this wretch is placed in the cell with all of the surgical equipment. You know the one?"*

The muscle-bound Vladimir smiled and nodded. *"And, Vladimir, see that Chelpinsky comes to no harm. I will carry out his interrogation personally, once I have been fixed up myself that is,"* said the President. He glanced down at all of the blood on his shirt, turned as white as a sheet, then promptly fainted.

As Vladimir started to undo the belts and ties securing them both, Chelpinski turned an even whiter shade of pale than the President and began whimpering. He knew just what was coming his way.

Ж

CHAPTER TWENTY ONE

'DOWN AT THE OLD DOG AND DUCK'

"Another pint, Mike?" asked Graham. *"Madness not to!"* said a smiling Mike. Nudging him, Graham said, *"Come on then, it's your round - don't be such a tightwad!"* said Graham. *"Your usual, Graham?"* asked Mike, sighing. *"Aye, a foaming pint of Timothy Taylor's Boltmakers, if you please, my good fellow,"* replied a smiling Graham.

Whilst Mike was stood at the bar waiting to be served, Graham picked up the Sunday newspaper that Mike had been reading and started leafing through the foreign news segment.

Suddenly he sat back and gasped, *"I don't pigging well believe it!"* Mike, who had returned with their drinks, asked him, *"You don't 'pigging well' believe what?"*

Graham tapped the newspaper with a trembling finger, *"Have you read this - the 'News from Russia' segment?"* Mike shook his head, *"No, I was just about to before you conned me into buying you a drink. What does it say?"*

Graham to a sip of his beer then said *"Sit down, I'll read it out to you:*

'President Baronovski was back at his desk inside the Kremlin yesterday after being elected to serve a second term in office.'

- and...." said Graham, pausing. *"And what?"* asked Mike impatiently.

Graham continued, *"And get this - his new Prime Minister is to be none other than the one and only, our friend and survivor, Igor Chel-bloody-pinski!"*

"Away with you man! Pass me that newspaper, let me have a look for myself!" said Mike. Graham handed the newspaper to him and Mike's eyes swept over the article. *"It cannae be the same man, surely!"* said Mike. *"It bloody well is - look at the photo underneath the article!"* said Graham, tapping the photo with his finger.

Beneath the article was a photograph of President Baronovski and Prime Minister Igor Chelpinsky, smiling and shaking hands, both of them looking extremely healthy and Baronovski proudly flashing a beautiful set of white teeth at the camera. *"Look at the Pres, stood there, grinning like Liberace!"* said Mike.

"So, looks like Baronovski had his gnashers fixed then," said Graham. *"Bloody hell,"* said Mike, *"he's got enough teeth in there for the both of us; looks as if he's breaking them in for a horse!"*

Shaking his head Mike said, *"I cannae believe it! Chelps - Prime Minister. The man has more lives than a cat!"* *"Just when we thought it was safe to go out at night,"* said Graham, *"and now this!"*

Mike sighed, *"We'd better get in touch with Ed De Jong and check that he knows about it, 'cos as sure as eggs are eggs, Chelps will be after him as well as the two of us. He's a vindictive little toe-rag."*

As they were chatting, unnoticed by them, the door at the front of the Dog and Duck Inn swung open and a nondescript middle-aged woman shuffled in. She made her way over to the bar and quietly ordered a vodka and tonic.

The nondescript woman ordered a drink then went and sat at a table. She attracted hardly any attention from the pubs clientele and sat there sipping her drink, fading into the background, as she'd been trained to do.

She surreptitiously opened her handbag and glanced inside it, just to reassure herself that the MP-443 Grach pistol that she'd collected from the Russian Embassy in London the previous day was nestling snugly at the bottom of her handbag, within easy reach.

Over in the far corner of the pub, Graham sighed and said to Mike, *"We're really going to have to watch our backs now, mate. Chelpinsky's a vindictive swine and he'll be sending some of his FSB lads after us!"* Mike nodded in agreement, *"Aye, you can put money on it!"*

The pub door swung open and a man's voice called out, *"Taxi for Mr Fraser!"* *"Be with you in a sec,"* shouted Mike. Mike turned to Graham and said, *"Come on G, drink up. I'll make that call to Ed on the way home."*

As the two men left the pub, the Rosa Klebb lookalike, (who was actually Major Natalia Preobrazhensky of the Russian FSB), placed the handbag in the crook of her arm then stood up and followed Mike and Graham, smiling to herself.

If she got the next bit right, Natalia had been promised immediate promotion to Lieutenant Colonel by no less a man than the Russian Prime Minister himself.

Mike and Graham clambered into the taxi and Graham said to the driver, *"If you could drop me off in Leconfield Village and then take my friend on to Hull, please."* The driver nodded. Mike looked across at him and said, *"Where's our usual driver then?"* The man turned to him and said, *"He's not very well. I was asked to stand in for him at the last minute."*

Suddenly the passenger door of the taxi swung open and Major Natalia Preobrazhensky jumped in beside the driver, slamming the door closed behind her. *"Er, excuse me Madam, I don't wish to be rude, but as you can see, this taxi is taken,"* said Mike.

Pulling the pistol out of her handbag, she turned to Mike and, pointing it at his chest, snarled, *"Shut up and both of you and keep your hands where I can see them. I have a message for you from the Russian Prime Minister."*

"Oh have you, and just who might you be?" asked Graham.

" I am Major Natalia Preobrazhensky!" "Oh right," said Mike, *"and would you mind spelling that for me, please?"* "Why?" asked a puzzled Natalya. *"So that I get it right when I pen my memoirs,"* said Mike, grinning.

The Major turned to the driver, *"Drive, Comrade Vyacheslav!"* The man asked, *"To Kingswood, Major?" "Of course, you fool - where else!"* she replied.

"Oh bloody hell fire, here we go again!" sighed Graham.

Ж

THE END

ABOUT THE AUTHOR

TERRY CAVENDER

After an enjoyable 30-year career in the British Army, Terry retired as a Major, then assumed an appointment with the Ministry of Defence for a further 18 years, latterly as a Media Operations Officer, until finally retiring. He has written, produced and directed several stage plays, pantomimes, films and plays for radio but now concentrates on writing fiction/faction.

Born in Keighley, West Yorkshire, Terry and his wife Maggie now live in faded gentility in the delightful market town of Beverley, East Yorkshire.

Terry has now started 'penning' his next book, its working title being – 'The House of Bread' - where the three key members of the 'Time-Team' have decided to jump on board the 'T3-Travellator' and travel back to the Middle-East to the year A.D. 36. What could possibly go wrong?

Printed in Great Britain
by Amazon